B.E.S.T. WORLD
SOME ASSEMBLY REQUIRED

Conclusion to
the B.E.S.T. World series

Cory McCarthy

Clarion Books
An Imprint of HarperCollinsPublishers

Clarion Books is an imprint of HarperCollins Publishers.

Library of Congress Control Number: 2023934379
ISBN 978-0-35-836215-9

Typography by Stephanie Hays
23 24 25 26 27 LBC 5 4 3 2 1

First Edition

TO YOU:

Augment your life any way you want.

—STEP ONE:

DEAL ———

ACE

1

TurboLegs v. SuperSoar

Nothing could wake Ace.

Not the pounding bass of his music, nor the exploding fireworks from his alarm clock, sizzling down the white glass walls of his bedroom. Not the *zip* of his big brother's TurboLegs in the hallway, or Mom yelling, "Finn! If you break the sound barrier *inside the house*, so help me!"

Not even Mama Jay sitting next to Ace, rubbing his back and saying his name, could wake him up. "Ace, kid. You're going to miss your Hyperloop. It's time for the last semester at ToP. This is the big one."

Ace closed his eyes tighter. "But what time is it?" he gurgled.

"Too early for someone mid–growth spurt. For the rest of us? Nine thirty."

That did it.

Ace had to be *on campus in position* at eleven on the dot. His heart thundered a sudden new tempo. He scrambled to his feet and nearly chased Mama Jay out of the room so that he could get dressed at light speed. He shoved the last few things he needed into his duffel and heaved it onto his shoulder, waddling into the kitchen under its significant weight.

He plopped down at the table and shoveled his bowl of eggs into his mouth, and then for good measure, his brother's bowl too. Mom was feeding Auto™ the dishes with one hand and reading a book in the other. He finished breakfast with a huge gulp.

The clock on the wall read 9:38.

"I'm going for the nine forty-five train. Byeloveyou!" Ace shot toward the door.

Mama Jay stepped in his path. She was wedging on the fingers of her weightlifting gloves. "Not so fast. Your moms have to talk to you about something."

"*Drudge!* I really want to get that train. I have . . . plans."

"Ace." Mom put her book down. "It'll take ten minutes to walk to the station, fifteen with your bag. You won't make that train."

"I'll run. Plus the train is always late this time of day. It'll be apex!"

"Your bag is *really* heavy. I suppose Finn could give you a hand."

"No thanks." The last thing Ace needed or wanted was anything from his big brother.

"What's your rush? You got a hot date?" Finn appeared in the doorway. Before Ace could growl at his teasing, Finn zipped to his chair and lifted his fork all in the same smug split second—except Ace had devoured Finn's eggs and the fork was one big empty bite. Finn's teeth clacked on it. "Did you eat my breakfast again? Mom!"

Mom snapped her fingers, and the kitchen bot started cooking more eggs.

"You know I'm having a growth spurt," Ace muttered, hoping it was true. He shoveled all his food in dutifully, but where did it go? He was only a pound heavier than when he'd started the program one and a half years ago. *One measly pound.*

"Faking a growth spurt, maybe," his brother joked. Mama Jay gave him a little poke, and he added, "I'm sure you're going to shoot up any day now."

Ace looked at his parents. He didn't even need to fake the big eyes. "I need to go."

Mama Jay put a gloved hand on his shoulder. "One second. It's your last semester. You've been patient and didn't rush into getting an aug earlier in the program like we asked, but before we consent to your surgery, you have to talk to us. Tell us why you've chosen the aug you've chosen."

Ace's face flamed. "You don't think I know what I want?

Or is this about the bad media?" He surprised himself with the sharpness of his tone. The Resistance had picked up in popularity over the last semester, which had made his moms want to pull him from the program—and yet even though Ace knew more about Bixonics's questionable methods than anyone in this house, he still wanted an aug more than (almost) anything. The only thing he wanted more was his friends' safety, but hey, wouldn't having an amazing aug help with that?

"Did Finn have to do this?" Ace sputtered.

Finn nodded. "Sorry, Deuce. Can't use the double-standard clause."

"But it's not *your* choice what aug I get!" Ace's temper lived right under his hair these days. It could flip out at any second.

Mom cleared her throat. "It's not our choice, and yet we're still going to talk to you about *your choices* because we love you. There's a lot of pressure at that program to become the flashiest new aug-bearer. We know you like SuperSoar, but . . . it's dangerous."

Finn held his bowl out and Auto™ served him hot eggs. "Trust me, little brother. Even if you could fly well enough to become a celebrity, you couldn't handle the hype. It's a lot of responsibility to be in the public eye."

Ace smiled thinly. What a grand, thoughtful state-ment. Even their parents were pleased. Finn seemed better at faking maturity these days. Ace wondered if that's all it took to be mature: learning how to fake it.

"We'd like you to promise to call *before* surgery," Mom said. "That's all."

He looked at his parents with genuine love but also with a small screaming voice inside. They were going to try to talk him out of his wings like everyone else. Wow, no one believed in Ace these days. He hugged his parents tight, unspoken anger ringing in his ears, then he grabbed his bag. "Okay, I'll call. Loveyoubye."

See? He was getting good at shoving his feelings. On second thought, maybe *that* was maturity. Finn seemed to run out of emotions about the same time he went to the Tower of Power and came home with a title: *Fastest Kid in the World*. Ace wondered if he cared about anything other than being a Bixonics celebrity these days.

Ace checked the time. He'd lost two precious minutes, which meant . . . *drudge*.

"Finn . . . Can you help me get my bag down to the station on time?"

"Maybe," his brother said coldly. "When I'm done eating my breakfast."

Ace ran out of the kitchen. Out of the house under a cloudy morning sky. The entire morning felt off, but not even that feeling could stop any of it from happening. Of course his brother wasn't going to help. And now *the plan* was in jeopardy.

Ace really needed to make that train.

He was already halfway down the steep road. Maybe the Hyperloop would be late. Maybe Ace was faster than people thought. Why was he the only one who had faith? It felt like all the boxmates were running downhill these days. Too fast to stop. Too fast to do anything but prepare for impact.

Unless, of course, he could fly.

While he ran, he leaped every few feet, his arms catching the wind, his body lifting. The duffel was too heavy to get any real air, but it didn't stop Ace from hurdling longer and higher, pushing up from the earth with every bit of spring in those thin-as-sticks legs.

At some point, someone would have to acknowledge what Ace had figured out: flying made sense for Ace. Because of SuperSoar, he wasn't the scrawniest kid at ToP; he had the perfect bird bones for soaring. The aug even required constant soaring and flapping—something can't-sit-still-Ace excelled at.

See? It was like Ace and SuperSoar were made-for-each-other.

There were more reasons. He had them all cataloged. Ready for the next person who asked him if he was *sure*. Or worse? If he was doing this to be like Finn.

The Hyperloop was pulling up, a little late just like he'd hoped. Ace was still too far away, but the train would wait two minutes with its doors open. He ran faster, faster, his leaps became huge. He really was flying.

The duffel caught the wind, and the whole thing swung forward. It pulled Ace off his feet and sent him rolling with his bag down the last part of the street. He got up, bruised and embarrassed, but still ready to get on board—which is when Finn appeared, blocking his way onto the Hyperloop platform.

The train doors began to close.

Ace nearly stampeded his brother, but Finn grabbed his duffel to stop Ace from getting on board, and Ace flipped that temper. He body-slammed his bag against his brother, and they both went down.

The train doors closed, and with a scream of wind, it was gone.

The empty Hyperloop shelter whirled with colorful Bixonics ads. Ace had bumped his noggin good, and even though he was angry, he had to take a minute to shake away the dizziness.

"What is wrong with you?" Ace hollered, jumping to his feet, fists balled. "I needed to get on board!"

Finn stretched his stupid, augmented calf muscles. "I was trying to toss your bag on *for you*. You know I could've got the doors before they closed. *You* are the reason you're not on that train right now."

Ace's mouth opened but then closed. This could be true. This could be a twisted truth. Something deeply alarming had happened over the last six months: Ace's brother had started being nice to him. On a semi-regular basis. For no reason.

Right? So suspicious.

Ace had even been going over all his brother's moves last night with Otis. Otis was still technically stuck in the elevator at ToP thanks to Bixonics's controlling software, but Jayla had made an elevator circuit board from Otis's own pieces, and linked them, and some other tech-y stuff. End result? Ace had a walkie-talkie with his bestie all program break, which was important seeing as how Gray and Jayla were always in Atlantis, scheming. And Leo, well . . .

The plan.

"When's the next train?" Ace asked.

Finn craned his head back to read the shelter's glass info board with its scrolling updates. "The next one isn't stopping. It's all full. Move-in day at ToP is a rough time to get downtown."

"When's the next train!"

"Ten forty-five."

Ace started pacing. His heart was hammering around his chest like Leo themself had given it a slam on the BESTBall court. "Finn, I have to get to ToP before eleven." He didn't have to add that the campus was at least a half hour on the Hyperloop.

Ace wasn't going to be in position on time.

Oh no, oh no.

Finn stretched, looked around. "I guess I could run

you there. Or are you too old for a piggyback, lil bro?"

Ace couldn't tell if Finn was teasing. Of course he was *too old*. Maturity-wise, Ace was ancient—and none of his family had even noticed! He'd been party to an underwater Resistance movement and knew secrets about Bixonics that his brother couldn't even imagine! But, technically, he wasn't *too big* for a piggyback.

"What about my duffel? You can't carry us both."

"Leave it. I'll zip you over and then I'll come back for it."

Ace smelled a trap, but he decided that—for Leo—he'd climb onto his brother's back like old times.

It was weird. Ace hadn't been physically close to his brother without punching or kicking in many years. His brother's clothes were so much nicer than Ace's, but then, they had the Bixonics logo stamped all over them, gifts from the company. Water and air resistant so that Finn could go fast and look good too.

His brother's entire life was a Bixonics ad.

Before he could *zip*, Ace cleared his throat. "Finn?"

"What?"

"Do you . . . trust Bixonics?"

"How can you trust a company?" He shifted Ace on his back. "A person you can trust. I trust our moms. I trust Dr. Bix." There was a raw softness in Finn's tone. Did his brother know that the famous scientist was chryo-frozen, poisoned by his own revolutionary formula, and replaced by the company with a sketchy holographic AI? Then again, Finn was always at those showy company gatherings. Maybe he did know that Dr. Bix was missing . . . or suspected it? "You shouldn't trust things that aren't alive, Ace. But I do trust Dr. Bix."

There was something about hearing his brother say it twice.

It made Ace admit it as well. "I trust Dr. Bix too."

"Also, what are you even talking about right now? You've wanted wings since you were a baby. Don't let the media buzz make you doubt yourself. Get your aug. Then make choices about who you work for or whatever."

Of all the people Ace had talked to about his aug choice—in some form or another over the last two years—this answer was closest to the one he wanted to hear.

Funnily enough, it didn't make him feel better.

"Ready? Hold *tight*. Moms will never forgive me if I drop you." Finn held Ace's legs tighter. His big brother too easily became the exact same guy who had lifted a five-year-old Ace onto his back and run around the yard. Finn had his birth legs then, but Ace had still thought his brother was faster than the Hyperloop. Finn would swing around until Ace's cape flew out from his shoulders like a superhero.

They called it *flying*.

Back when they were friends.

Ace had forgotten that until just this second.

Finn sprinted without warning. It was like falling

hard—*and* sideways. At first, Ace couldn't do anything but feel his face flap, and then a breath later, he was sort of enjoying it. From the satellite feeds of Finn, he always looked like his speed was constant, but from this viewpoint, Ace could tell that Finn had to watch which way he was going. He slowed and turned a lot. He went up and down mountains. Across the surface of lakes. For the first time, Ace realized that his brother ran over showy landscapes not to show off, but because there were fewer people, and he could go faster.

Ace *supposed* that explained it.

Downtown's outline swelled on the horizon in no time. The sun was coming up on his back, but he knew they were making incredible time. His brother's legs really were something special. And didn't that hurt to admit.

Finn stopped too fast, and Ace's head spun when he was dropped to the ground. "Jeez, you're tiny! I could barely feel you back there. Like a little bug on my shoulder."

Ace reddened. "Yeah, well, it wasn't a blast for me either."

"Come on, you loved it when we used to fly together."

So his brother *did* remember.

Ace dug deep inside and found that connection they once had. "Okay, maybe it was cool to feel you run so fast. Too bad you can't get VisionX. Seems like the only thing holding your speed back is not being able to see farther ahead."

Finn stared at his brother. "No one can have two augs, Deuce. Why do you spend so much time imagining things that can't happen? You're never going to be more mature until you get *real*." He had an edge to his voice, like his kindness had run out. And there was a small audience gathering around the place where he'd zipped in, fans ready to mingle with the mascot for Bixonics, as if Finn had appeared just to entertain.

Someone actually cried out, "Look! The Fastest Kid in the World!"

Fastest drudge, maybe. Ace's butt was indeed on the jeweled tile of the campus courtyard, so he supposed his brother had held up his end of the bargain, but he also needed his bag. "Can you go get my duffel before you hang out with your fans?"

"I told you I would get it. Give me a minute." Finn started signing autographs. Experience promised that this would take a lot longer than a minute.

"Well, I need it now, Finnegan. I told you. *I have plans.*"

Finn glared at him, handed back the toddler he'd been taking a picture with, and *zap.* The crowd cheered like usual when he sprinted off, although Ace supposed his brother had never once been able to hear it. He was always miles ahead.

The courtyard grew crowded as cadets and caregivers disembarked from the Hyperloop in the hundreds. A new security fence rimmed the base of ToP. Hercules-augged guards held the perimeter and kept protesters from entering the colorful square. Ace almost didn't notice that there was a secondary security team of people with the aug FelineFinesse. They'd climbed the surrounding decorative trees and signage, tails swinging gently while their diamond-shaped pupils searched the crowd for trouble.

The streaming screen ads for Bixonics lit up the large tiles beneath Ace's butt, and he jumped because they'd all linked into one enormous image—and he was sitting on Leo's digital eyebrow. Ace hadn't seen Leo or even talked to them since they'd been wheeled off to surgery. He tried not to remember that miserably sad conference in the Otis, all three boxmates ready to save them . . . only to be too late.

This ad was a handsome picture of them, complete with BESTBall under the arm and their sleek new chair in Bixonics green. Not to mention the Sherlock smirk. That's what Jayla called the "I know two moves ahead of everyone" smirk. Over the last semester, Leo had become the poster kid for Bixonics's Sherlock campaign, and now it was the aug *everyone* wanted, though it was still nearly impossible to get approved to try it out.

A shadow fell over Ace. Coach Vaughn looked down at him, backlit with his sunnies on. "Coach! You're back!"

"I didn't go anywhere." His voice was the perfect combo of familiar and gruff.

"Yes you did! You weren't here all last semester. I sent

you so many messages. Otis and I spied on your house. I miss—" Ace had nearly told his old coach that he'd missed him. Was that weird? Nah. Maybe?

Vaughn grinned. Oh right, Ace didn't have to put his feelings into words around this guy. He got it. "Missed you too, kid, but I was *on vacation*."

"A vacation where you didn't have email and didn't say goodbye to anyone?"

Vaughn's look made it clear that there was more information, and Ace wasn't going to get it right now. Ace tried on patience. It didn't fit well.

"On your feet, Wells." He offered Ace a hand, and Ace shot to his feet with Coach's help. "Oof, haven't hit that growth spurt yet, huh?"

Vaughn's words splattered all over Ace's feelings. Like bird poop.

"Skinny is key for SuperSoar," he muttered sourly.

"I apologize. That was thoughtless of me." Vaughn looked genuinely worried, and Ace didn't like it. He told his feelings to give the coach's iNsight aug, aka the empathy enhancer, a clear message: change the subject.

Instead, his brother reappeared with his duffel and dropped it *on* his feet.

"You're welcome!" Finn scoffed in a rush and zipped off again, although not away. He did a few whooshing circles around the courtyard and then stopped in the center of the people he'd herded and bowed for their applause.

Ace sort of howled, his toes smashed. "Even when he's nice he's foul!"

Coach Vaughn chuckled. "You just need some space. Space is healthy. You'll be here, and he'll be home. Though I guess a lot has changed around here while I was on vacation, if you're getting rides to campus with Finn."

"I just missed my train and I've got . . . stuff to do. So he helped."

"Stuff to do. Upperclassmen responsibilities or practical jokes with Otis?"

Ace grinned. It was too awesome to have Vaughn back. That had to be a good sign. Last semester had not been the same. No Jayla, Leo. At least Gray had been a grad aug, and they got to hang out sometimes, but it wasn't the same. That first semester had been something special with all the boxmates together and Coach looking out for him.

Otis played back security footage all the time. Ace had gotten a little addicted to watching it like a TV show. The boxmates fooling around in the zero gravity of the labyrinth. Cheering together at Leo's games, faces bright green. Movie night and video game sprees . . . the box just bursting with laughter.

Would he ever get to have that again?

Ace looked at his old coach longingly. "Want to come up to the Coliseum and see how many flaps I can get in with SuperSoar? I haven't been able to practice all break, but I bet I can do at least fifteen minutes. I've improved a lot since you disappeared . . ." Vaughn looked at him exasperatedly. "On vacation?"

Ace dropped a pin in Vaughn's weird "vacation." Otis would talk it through with him later, no doubt.

"Can't play now. It's orientation, Wells. I've got a whole batch of newbs to show around." Coach held out his roster, and Ace had a flash of meeting him a year and a half ago. It felt like twenty lifetimes. He was suddenly kind of sad to be too old to be one of Vaughn's cadets. "But I thought you had stuff to do, Mr. Flying Ace?"

"Oh! Right." Ace was so happy to be back beneath the campus's three-hundred-story jeweled skyscraper that he'd nearly forgotten that he still needed to be ready by eleven. He checked his tablet. Only twenty-four minutes to get what he needed and get in position . . . on the roof of the Tower of Power.

And the best part? By the end of today, not a single person on this planet would be able to doubt that Ace could fly.

JAYLA

2

Brilliance v. Exhaustion

[data correction entered: ready to try again?]

Jayla nodded, and her network swirled into action. Her eyes were peeled on the streaming lines of code that projected from the interface on her arm.

It was early in the Resistance Research Lab of Atlantis, deep in the Pacific Ocean. The other workstations were empty, and the berry-blue glow of her network was the only spot of brilliance on this dim, undersea level. The large round portholes looking out into the sea were black as night, flecked with bioluminescence instead of stars.

Jayla doubted her parents were awake yet; she had needed to be up too early for her part in *the plan*, and it had originally seemed like a great idea to stay awake all night and get some work done. Plus, she'd had a real eureka moment sometime around two in the morning and that third, electrifying can of ZAPP. What if today was the day they saved Leo *and* she cured Bixonium poisoning?

Stranger things had happened to the boxmates.

So far Jayla had only found a lot of ways to *not* cure the lethal dose of Dr. Bix's formula that he had accidentally infected himself and his wife with. Every few days, Jayla visited their chryo-tubes on the medical level, reminding herself that this was more important than hanging out with the parents she was still patching things up with after running away to get augged. Or crushing on Amir. She'd promised Grayson she'd save his parents, and she would keep that promise.

Jayla flicked her fingers through the program, making it scroll faster. She'd created this app to assess every possible counter formula, testing her latest theory with lightning speed. Although, honestly, her network was running slow, which meant Jayla was nearly too tired to run it. She drank the last of her ZAPP and felt the program speed up a tiny bit.

She checked the time. She had twenty-three minutes before she needed to be in position, ready to help Ace. Her finger hovered over her interface, unable to pause the processing because it was doing one of those satisfying bursts, going from 81% complete to 99%.

"Come on, come on," she whispered.

Instead of a result review for her serum, a very different screen interrupted everything.

[energy alert: 20% remaining before uncon-sciousness]

"Noooo," Jayla cried. She went rummaging around her workstation, searching for nourishment. Fuel. Instead, she encountered an embarrassing number of power bar wrappers and empty energy beverage cans. At this point, she'd even drink from one of Ace's ocean coconuts.

The sharp memory from nearly a year ago made her snort.

Jayla finally found the butt end of a candy bar and ate it. Within a minute, her energy level went above the danger zone, just a little, but enough. She cleared the warning, trying to get back to finishing the 1% of the program, but her network interrupted again.

[calendar alarm: twenty minutes before *the plan*]

"Drudge!" She flung off her lab coat, limbs heavy, and jogged to the elevator. Okay, maybe she had done it again: traded her brilliance for a "uniquely stupid level of exhaustion," to quote her dad. She could hear her parents now, deep in the back of her mind, telling her that the most world-altering scientists took naps.

"I'll sleep when I've fixed the world," she grumbled. She pressed the elevator button no fewer than seventeen times. When it opened, she squeezed in blindly, surprised to be surrounded by an entire group of her peers in bathing suits, headed to the swim level, no doubt.

Amir and his one-dimple-smile was one of them.

He waved hello, and she tucked in beside him.

"That's *Jayla*, isn't it?" someone whispered behind her.

Someone else added, "She's our age but she works for the Resistance, like her parents."

"She's the one who made sure Bixonics can't track us," another voice added.

Jayla tried to feel proud of her reputation—and success—but instead she yawned so big she made an involuntary sound like a small lion.

"Why are you all going swimming in the middle of the night?" she blurted at Amir.

"Swim team. We practice at five in the morning."

"Oh, right." She'd forgotten that she was on the ToP time zone, trying to stay linked in with *the plan*. She also forgot that some teens got to do things like team sports and have fun.

Jayla had no idea that she'd fallen asleep standing up, head sunk on Amir's shoulder, until he gave her a little shake. The swim team had disembarked the elevator, but the door was still open and the smell of the saltwater pool was making her remember ToP longingly.

"Going home?" Amir was reaching for the button for the level where Jayla lived with her folks. She pushed his hand away and used her network to input her real destination: the seafloor.

"You're taking a tender topside?" Concern carved lines on Amir's face. "By yourself? In this state?"

"I have an important—" This yawn was bigger than a grown-up lion's. "Mission."

"Sounds like you could use a pilot," he offered.

She shook her head, but she did need a pilot.

[energy alert: 10% remaining before unconsciousness, entering low power mode]

"Drudge," she cursed blearily. "Do you have chocolate, Amir?"

"Always." He smiled, one hand on her shoulder, holding her upright. "But I think what you really need is sleep."

It was as if that one little word was a command, and she would have dropped to the floor of the elevator if he hadn't had one arm around her shoulders.

"LEO!" Jayla yelled, sitting upright.

She expected to be in her bed, having completely blown the plan to save her beloved boxmate. Instead she was depressurizing in a small tender, on her way to the ocean's surface.

Amir was piloting. He still wore his swim trunks and a T-shirt, and Jayla had the weirdest flash like they were going to hang out topside and go swimming and get some sun like the world wasn't precariously balanced between Bixonics tyranny and Resistance revolution.

"A few minutes and we'll be topside. Your network completely unplugged. You know, I don't think I've ever gotten mine so low. Must take talent to keep working with no brain cells available." He handed her a banana. She glared at it. "Eat that first. I have water and chocolate in my bag."

She eyed Amir. "How do you know how low on power I am? Did you run diagnostics on me?"

"Oh, it's way more sinister than that. You *never* rest. You're almost always too low on power."

Jayla peeled the banana and chewed, trying to swallow as much of it in as few bites as possible. After that, she drank all the water and ate every bit of chocolate that Amir had in his bag.

"Don't tell me I shouldn't let it get so low," she growled.

"Did I?"

"No, but I could feel you thinking it."

"You can feel what I'm thinking?" His smirk was kind of beautiful. Was she staring? "You got a secret iNsight aug you want to tell me about?" Amir said things like that sometimes, like he was about to see if they were friends who were saving the world together . . . or more-than-friends who were saving the world together.

Either way, it was a lot of distraction from saving the world.

So was the half a bar of chocolate that Jayla was trying to swallow all at once. After she'd re-upped her energy input, she put her head back and closed her eyes. It meant missing Amir's underwater piloting and the spectacular view of the ocean through the front window, but she was *very* tired, whether she liked it or not.

There was a small voice in the back of her head that wondered how long she could do this all on her own. Maybe she should ask her dad to help her with the formula. Or her mom. They certainly wanted to, but they were busy with their own essential missions. Her mom was singlehandedly running the Resistance, and thanks to Jayla, her dad was now booked solid monitoring all the newly un-tracked augs in Atlantis. Everyone had a job in defeating Bixonics, and Jayla felt rather solemn about the vow she'd made to Grayson to save his parents.

Though, she should really be thinking about Leo right now.

Gray was somewhere far away, also getting into position, heading up in the space elevator to Bixonics HQ all by himself . . . Ace would be getting ready to pull his fake out stunt. All such important things to think about—and yet Jayla completely conked out through depressurization.

She woke much more gently this time to the bright yellow sunlight of the ocean's surface beneath a pristine blue sky. Amir was shaking her shoulder. The tender bobbed lightly on the gentle rolling waves. In the distance, she could make out the little island of the guard shack where Rosa and Stern manned the top of Atlantis, keeping a watchful eye out for anything Bixonics.

[energy alert: 30% power, calendar alarm: three minutes until *the plan*]

Jayla felt a surge of information as her network linked

with the global satellites that waited just outside the protection of Atlantis, the only real security the Resistance had at staying camouflaged—and active—right under Bixonics's nose. Jayla herself had revolutionized the process of untethering augged folks from the company, but even that was risky.

At some point, Bixonics was going to catch on. And what would they do then? Punish Atlantis? Try to shut it down? The Resistance was big these days, growing in popularity everywhere. Getting perhaps *too much* media attention, her dad kept saying.

Okay. Too many things to think about. Jayla needed to focus.

She sent a code to Ace. Well, to Otis, but that was how to reach Ace these days.

Amir was quiet but paid attention to her every move. He helped boost her signal with his own network, sort of piggybacking the message she sent out.

"I can't tell if it's reached him and he can't respond, or if it didn't reach him."

Jayla risked a verbal signal. "Otis, pal? You out there? Is Ace in position?"

After a fuzzy moment, Otis sang back. "Knock, knock."

She pinched the bridge of her nose with two fingers. "Are you serious?"

"Never," the elevator AI promised.

"Otis!" Ace's voice piped in. "This is important!"

"Ace! Why are you not on the roof?" Jayla yelled. "Gray will be in position *any minute*."

"I am! I'm using the Otis-walkie you made for me. I'm ready to fly!"

"Don't even think about it!" Jayla's heart thundered as her network found Ace, pinging off satellites. She projected the image into the small, bobbing tender for Amir to watch as well. At first it was the swirled blue and white and occasionally ground-spotted Earth. Then the view zoomed to the continent, and then downtown, and then to the gleaming Tower of Power.

She had strange pangs looking at it. This had been Jayla's home for a year and a half—where she came into her own and created her own network to rival Bixonics's itself. This was also where she missed her parents and worried that they might never want to see her again. Of course they always would, how could she have ever thought that?

She dialed in closer to the tiny image of Ace next. The view spun around him showing off his SuperSoar trial wings, standing on the roof of the three-hundred-story building. The wind pulled at his hair in a way that made Jayla nervous. As if he could sense the satellite camera, he grinned and gave a thumbs-up.

Could the wind just toss him over?

She clicked on the audio connection again. "Ace. You're really close to the edge. Remember, this is supposed to be a publicity stunt in their eyes. You keep yourself tethered to reality *and* that roof."

There was a longer pause than usual. Almost like Ace didn't have one of his ready-fire answers. "This is going to work." Even his tone was a little defensive.

"Are you tethered? I can't see where it's connected to you."

"I have it."

But he didn't have it on. Jayla muted the connection. "Great. All our hopes rest with an AI with a low-quality sense of humor and Mr. Desperate-to-SuperSoar." As soon as she said it, she wished she hadn't. That was the problem with getting so tired. She was turning into a grump. "I didn't mean that."

Amir nodded understandingly. "This morning I yelled at my mom because I couldn't find my own trunks. We're all nervous that Bixonics is about to do something."

"Well." Jayla cracked her knuckles and readied the interface on her arm. "They're not doing anything first. We've got all the cards here."

Amir crossed his arms. "So . . . Ace is going to *pretend* to jump off the roof? As a ruse? I don't see the logic in it."

"I know. But we wanted to let Ace make up his own part of the plan. He's always trying to make wings 'a thing.' Even when we were in the box just getting takeout, he'd be like, 'Too bad I can't just fly over . . .' He's completely convinced that at some point, we're all going to need those wings to save the world."

"I'd watch that movie." Amir smiled at her. One deep dimple on one cheek. He showed her that dimple too much. She was starting to like it too much.

Jayla wanted to trust Ace; it was just . . . hard. She focused on the plan and sent the feed of Ace on the roof to all the big communications corporations on the planet, even to Leo's twin sister, Emma, with her silly ToP gossip show. "Here comes the circus, Ace!"

Within minutes, the roof was buzzing with drone cameras and helos. She switched views to a streaming news feed, the media coverage heightened by the recent rise in what had been dubbed "Bixonics Resistance."

Jayla watched as one of the more famous newscasters' holos projected on the roof right in front of Ace.

The reporter stuck his gold-plated holographic mic right under Ace's nose. "Cadet, can you tell us what's going on right now?"

"I'm about to fly off this roof, that's what's going on! I'm the first cadet to ever successfully use the SuperSoar wings!"

Jayla put a flat hand over her face. "Oh no."

"Are you sure that's safe?" the reporter asked. "Are you making a statement on behalf of the Bixonics Resistance?"

Ace turned a little green. He stuttered but no words came out.

"Oh jeez," Jayla muttered.

Amir squinted at the image filling the small tender. "Is anyone else annoyed that they keep saying 'Bixonics Resistance'? Like even the name of *our* group has to have the B-word in it?"

Jayla fussed with the signal. It kept freezing and fuzzing. Maybe they weren't far enough away from the satellite blocker. Or maybe Bixonics was messing with the feed. "Honestly? I always thought 'Resistance' was a strange angle. I think we're more like absolute rebels."

Amir linked his network with Jayla's, and together, the image unfroze.

They were rather powerful together. He gave her another one of those beautiful smirks.

"Thanks." Jayla had done her part of the plan, but it felt wrong to sit back and watch. Ace wasn't alone on the roof. Lots of the ToP coaches were up there now. And actual reporters were dropping in from helos, their harnesses barely wrinkling their fancy suits.

"Well," Amir started, "Ace was right that this would get a lot of attention. Look at that! It's on every channel, streaming globally. I think there are over a billion people tuned in to watch!"

"Yeah, well, as long as he doesn't actually try to fly off that roof. He'll break a lot more than both of his legs this time."

The moment the words left Jayla's lips, she knew that was probably going to happen. Even worse? There was a

ZIP in the streaming image. Ace's big brother Finn had showed up and immediately tried to drag him away from the edge.

It was a full-on brawl . . . on a three-hundred-story ledge.

"Come on, Grayson," Jayla whispered like a prayer. "Don't let all this be for nothing . . ."

A message interrupted Jayla's network. It came through Amir's as well, since they were linked. He looked at it, then at her.

Jayla could only stare at the words.

[processing 100% complete: antiserum compound successful, Bixonium degraded in virtual patient X]

GRAYSON

3

Leo v. Gray

Grayson was on a literal elevator to space.

One wall was glass, showing off a spectacular view of the world falling beneath him. Two miles away. Maybe three now. He used his aug eyes to peer down, and while he could make out the rainbow skyscraper of ToP easily enough, he couldn't see if Ace was in position on the roof. Or if any part of this plan was even working.

He just had to trust that everyone was doing their part, so he could do his.

Gray had been up this elevator at least a dozen times before, when he was smaller, side by side with his dad. When his ears popped and his feet started to feel lighter in his shoes—just like they had back then—Gray was struck by a memory that made his VisionX eyes water.

This will be your lab someday, Dr. Lance Bix had once said in this very elevator. *This whole company will be yours.*

Gray had had distant feelings about that even when he was eight years old, before his time in the program changed everything. Before his boxmates became his friends *and* family—while his parents were taken away by the very formula that had made them all beyond rich, beyond powerful.

No matter the controlling, evil trajectory of the company, the Bix name still carried weight. But how much? He didn't know, although he was testing that theory right now . . .

Ever since Gray had been too late to save Leo from the Sherlock aug surgery, he'd been waiting for this moment: seeing them again. Rescuing them from Bixonics's controlling grip, not unlike the way Jayla had freed him.

It had been six painful months of silence. So many unanswered messages. He'd even gone to Leo's house and had dinner with their parents. He'd done interviews with Emma for her gossip feed, just to hear the scraps of messages that Leo had sent home from their new position on the edge of space, in Bixonics HQ.

Decades earlier, this place had been called the International Space Station.

Gray's dad had bought the abandoned floating piece of space junk from the government and renovated it when Gray was still toddling around. Dr. Bix had turned it into a safe place to handle the Bixonium formula.

With a jolt, Gray realized that his dad must have

suspected even back then that large amounts of the stuff were not safe for people to be around. Gray only wished he'd figured that out even earlier, before it had cost his dad so much.

And his mom.

He couldn't think about them now. Jayla was creating a cure, and she had never failed at anything. He took a deep breath and looked back out the window to the ever-distant Earth. He had to trust; it was hard.

One of the truly cool things his dad had done with the defunct space station was build this state-of-the-art elevator made of cables as thick as bathtubs—although for a speeding piece of technological innovation, this was taking forever.

He glanced at the Bixonics security detail on either side of him. Both clearly had Hercules augs. He'd never needed to be accompanied before. Maybe the gaining popularity of the Resistance was changing things. Although, honestly, it felt like Bixonics was more dangerous than ever. Like a wounded animal.

He checked the time on his watch.

11:01. *Oh, drudge.*

He was late.

The elevator finally dinged. It was a lifeless sound, and it almost made him miss the way Otis never let any trip, up or down, remain unmemorable. The doors opened, and Gray was a little alarmed to find even more security guards in green Bixonics uniforms mingling in the lobby, waiting for him.

There was some artificial gravity up here, but not as much as on Earth. Gray's steps felt lighter than usual as he walked into the foyer. This place didn't feel like his dad's exciting space lab anymore. The company had turned it into something very different, an off-planet headquarters where things like tax laws and human rights regulations didn't exist. A place where Bixonics could do whatever they needed to do without anyone being able to stop them.

Well, almost anyone.

Gray's insta-grin nearly exploded his face.

Leo wheeled toward him at top speed. Gray pushed the guards out of the way to give them a hug, lifting them several inches out of their chair. Leo laughed lightly in his arms, squeezing him around the neck.

"Can't believe you came all the way up here!" they muttered in his ear.

"Don't worry," he tried to say. "We have a—"

Oof.

Leo's elbow dug straight into his side. At the same time, a rather clipped voice said, "Hello, Grayson. I wonder . . . Do you remember me?"

Gray looked over at a man about Coach Vaughn's age, though his hair was streaked with silver and his eyes wore shadowy bags. Gray was shocked to recognize his dad's old assistant. "Mr. Danvers? What are you doing here? I thought you . . ."

"Lost my mind? Hardly. I've had such bad press as one of the first Sherlocks. It's almost like they *want* me to be Moriarty." He chuckled. "To be honest, I'm not mad at it."

"He's my boss," Leo said, matter-of-factly.

Gray knew that Leo was up here with members of the Bixonics company board, but he was not expecting Felix Danvers. "Leo, he's a Sherlock. And he's . . . unwell."

Leo actually grinned oddly. "*I'm* a Sherlock. Is it unwell to know more than other people? I suppose it might seem that way from the outside."

Gray felt a little cold. These didn't feel like Leo's words—it felt more like a puppet master was pulling their strings. Leo didn't make grand statements. They moved in silence most of the time, saving their words for the right moment.

But then, it had been a year since they'd been together. Maybe Leo was different now.

Maybe being a Sherlock changed them.

Mr. Danvers was pleased by this warm-to-cool inter-action. He cupped his hand and motioned for both to follow, leading the way deeper into the station, toward a room that held a mighty oak desk. The picture window behind it looked out over the entire planet. Show-off.

Danvers took a seat, and Leo wheeled into a spot for their chair beside him. "I'm so intrigued by your offer to support the company during this time of minor chaos, Grayson."

Oh, Felix Danvers thought that the Resistance was "minor chaos."

Little did he know.

"Gray is good, actually."

Danvers ignored him. "When we received your message, Leo and I were tickled. We spent a good few days working through all your possible ulterior motives. It was so much fun!"

He looked to Leo, and they smiled back. This was *not* one of Leo's smiles. Not the triumphant "I just scored on the BESTBall court" smile. Not the shy one with the blush. Not even the smirk that Jayla had dubbed the "I know two moves ahead of everyone" smirk.

This was new.

Fake?

Mr. Danvers was downright smug. It reminded Gray of someone familiar he couldn't put his finger on. "What did we end up deciding, Leo?"

"Rescue attempt," they answered without emotion.

"Oh yes. Definitely cute, but an ultimately poorly developed scheme to get Leo away from here. Little do you know, this is the only place where Leo is safe."

If Gray had felt cold before, he was downright chilled now.

What was worse, Leo had no reaction to any of this.

"All silly childish schemes aside, I was hoping you could tell me how your dad is doing. It's been an awfully long time since he's come up here to visit. I'm starting to wonder if he's the one who is *unwell*."

Gray knew that everything about his mannerisms and words would tell this dangerous person too much. That's what the Sherlock aug did: heightened one's powers of deduction. "He's doing . . . okay."

"Alive, is he?" Mr. Danvers looked at his hands. "Not to sound unkind, but I just didn't imagine he would make it this long. I did wonder if he could pass away without anyone noticing how dangerous his formula can be. That would be quite the trick."

Gray wondered if lies would even help here. Couldn't the aug see through them? Would he accidentally give away too much by trying to hide what was happening? He looked to Leo and realized that they didn't know about his dad frozen on the med level in Atlantis. How could they? They were stuck at ToP when he'd finally learned the truth about his parents' conditions . . .

"He's sick, but he's alive." His eyes flashed to Leo's, and finally, he saw the spark of the person he knew so well. His best friend. They were in there somewhere, hiding.

It was only a flash, and then it was gone. Leo seemed to retreat behind a curtain.

Mr. Danvers continued, carefully wording the next bit. "It does seem that when the famed scientist goes the way of Marie Curie, it'll be time for you to take up the mantle, won't it? I thought that allowing you to come up here for a visit might help us get on good terms. I'd like us to be partners in Bixonics's future."

"I haven't decided if I'm going to head the company yet," Grayson said quickly. What he wanted to say was *Oh, I'd rather burn it all down, thanks.* "My dad is going to get better, so none of that is going to really matter."

Mr. Danvers was examining every word, deducing. He was also retreating inside his brain. His eyes went a bit cloudy, and the rest of his words came out strange.

"*Interesting.* But I am a human of my word, and I offered you an opportunity to hang out with my young star pupil while you shoot a commercial for your augs." He chuckled. "And don't we need the publicity." He touched the back of Leo's hand, a quick pat that Gray swore Leo nearly recoiled from. "Leo, show him to the court I made for you. I'll make sure the director is ready to roll camera."

"Can I show Gray my room?" Leo asked.

"Oh, I don't think so." His eyes were so cloudy now that he seemed like a zombie. He flicked his hand, and Leo wheeled out from behind the desk. They grabbed Gray's wrist and gave it a tug. Gray couldn't really take his eyes away from the blurry-eyed person with the sagging posture.

Mr. Danvers was sick too. From Bixonium poisoning.

Gray would have recognized those symptoms any-where. With a shiver he realized he might have just met the wounded animal inside Bixonics.

Leo's "boss."

Leo wheeled slightly ahead of him. Gray had to walk fast. He woke up from the trance of finding Leo with his father's former assistant when he remembered that Jayla and Ace were depending on him. Jayla would be out of the safety of Atlantis, bobbing on the ocean, and Ace was on an actual, honest-to-augs rooftop.

The Bixonics guards trailed them but didn't come too close.

"I think you're a bigger shot in this company than me now." He nodded back toward the security detail. "Can you get rid of them?"

"They're here to make sure I'm safe."

"Why aren't you safe?"

Leo didn't respond or even slow down until they'd reached what had to be the farthest end of the station. They opened the door with an iris scan. Gray stepped into an impressive, albeit small, BESTBall court. At least it was empty of Bixonics employees. They entered while the detail stayed outside.

"Felix had this built for me." Leo wheeled to a rack of BESTBalls. "He wants me to be happy up here. He's been good, not too unstable, although rigorous sometimes with his mental challenges." They touched their temple like the words made a memory ache.

"Leo . . ." Gray's voice said a lot of emotional things in that one word.

They shook their head. "Everything is being recorded. *Everything*. He'll watch it over and over later, and he'll probably punish me for telling you this much." Leo looked up into thin air, spoke to it. "I had to. Grayson doesn't understand our aug."

"I have to get you out of here." For the first time in his entire life, Gray had a flash of being head of this company like his dad—and the first thing he would do was rescue Leo from whatever this space prison had turned out to be.

Leo shot a ball at Gray, and it hit his chest, causing a loud *oof*. "It's not a prison. More like a boot camp." They must have deduced Gray's thoughts; it was a little unnerving how close they were to the mark. "And I need it. This aug makes me feel like one of Ace's all-powerful superheroes, and not always in a good way."

Gray shot the ball back, hard. "So you're trying not to become a supervillain?"

"Think of it this way. Sherlock was new when Felix got it. He didn't have anyone to learn from, and he got a bit . . . overwhelmed. He designed a training program for this aug, and I think we can both agree that there can be good Sherlocks, with help."

"What about Rosa?" Gray asked.

"Rosa is dead. And that's a tragedy." There was a threat for caution in Leo's tone. Gray had to admit that he wasn't very good at talking around the facts. He'd forgotten that the Resistance had faked Rosa's death in order to buy her freedom.

"Rosa was a big loss for Felix. Don't bring it up again." Leo paused. "His grief has become old anger. He won't fail me the way he lost her."

Before Gray could figure out how to respond to that, a team of Bixonics employees poured in. They peppered Leo's hair and face with combs and makeup, before coming at him. Gray checked the urge to swat them all away. Leo's eyes were on his in an intense way.

Staring, staring. Saying something?

Gray had the feeling that he was supposed to do or know something, but what?

They smirked at his bewilderment. Technically Gray's eyes were the same color after his aug surgery, but there was a sheen that made them almost metallic. Leo was taking in the change with startling intensity. "With your VisionX eyes, can you see all kinds of stuff, like temperature fluctuations?"

"I can see a range of heat waves, sure." Why was Leo asking him this? They knew all that stuff about how VisionX worked, didn't they? Was this . . . flirting? "I wouldn't, umm, look at anyone's body temperature without their permission."

Now Leo was blushing. And it made Gray feel warm all over. Leo added, "I meant that sometimes my wheels burn the court so fast that the rubber leaves heat smears. I was wondering if you could see it."

Gray knew they were saying something important, but what? "Maybe. I'll try."

The commercial director stepped between them. Gray would've recognized this role anywhere; he'd done so many Bixonics ads in his life. The person started to bark orders and point. "Now, you two, I want some real organic shots. You play, and we'll see what we have to work with. I've been promised you have dynamic chemistry!"

Gray glanced at Leo and all the warm in his body turned hot. "Just play?" he croaked.

Leo bounced a BESTBall off Gray's stunned chest. He nearly didn't catch it. Within seconds, Leo was zooming around the abridged court, scoring twice before Gray realized that he was supposed to be playing too. The milder gravity didn't seem to hold them back at all but made them even more streamlined.

Watching Leo play dazed him. He was so impressed with their ease on the court. He almost forgot to use his VisionX like Leo asked, and when he blinked three times to turn on the temperature sensors, the court radiated with scratches of heat from Leo's rubber wheels, just like they thought.

And Leo had written a message:

X = AI

Gray tried not to gape. What did that mean?

"No, no. Cut!" the director yelled. "We need your augs in action. Grayson, let's get a good close-up on those shimmering, zooming eyes." The director snapped their fingers at the camera bot. "Get an angle where we can *see* Leo coming up on him, reflected in those pretty irises. BEST-Ball about to score. The threat of a collision. Yes, that will be electric!"

Leo took the notes with an expression of annoyance that reminded Grayson of their earlier times together. It was a relief. The camera bot fussed up and down, left and right, trying to get the shot.

Grayson's vision mode was still registering heat waves as he looked at Leo. They blushed so hard when Gray looked directly at them. They had for years. Gray didn't need an aug to see that, but he didn't know when he was supposed to say something about it. They'd been friends for so long. Sometimes it felt like they'd always just be friends. But then, during their last few months together at ToP, they were inseparable in the box, and Leo had gotten more patient with each trial aug while his dad grew less. "I missed you," Gray blurted out, the words loud. Sure of himself.

Leo blushed harder, and he could tell it was too much for their shyness, and yet they were forcing themself to look at him. Leo tossed the ball at his head . . . hard. He caught it, but only just. Then they both laughed.

"Cut!" The director took the ball from Gray, who was

memorizing the letters from the floor as they faded. Before they could even give it back to Leo to restart the shot, the entire crew became wrapped up in breaking news. Everyone was glued to a broadcast on their watches and tablets.

Gray would have recognized the little image anywhere: Ace on the roof of ToP, wearing the SuperSoar trial wings—and having a full-on brawl with his brother, Finn. The crew was cursing, gasping. Someone blew the image up to a holograph form and put it in the center of the group.

"Oh . . . no." Gray was staring at a life-size version of the events atop ToP.

"Gray," Leo murmured. It was the first time he'd heard their soft, shy voice since he'd come up here. Their real voice. "Ace is going to fall."

Gray's heart thundered. The certainty with which Leo said that made him feel like it had already happened. Was that what it was like to live with Sherlock? To know the future? He had an instinct to run for the door, but how in the world would he get there fast enough to help his boxmate? Everyone gasped as Ace kicked hard to get out of his brother's grip—and fell right over the safety rail, and over the ledge.

The media feed followed him down, down via drone camera. Leo's hand slipped into Gray's. Ace was a tumble of wings, unable to flap, turning head over feet. He was trying so hard to get his arms in the right position, but he was in complete, chaotic freefall.

Plummeting.

Ace didn't hit the courtyard below, though.

Finn zoomed into place just in the nick of time and caught him, turning all that momentum into a circular sprint around the courtyard. Finn tossed Ace down and bowed to his fans, holding one of his arms as though he'd hurt it badly. All the caregivers and newbs erupted in riotous applause. Even the crew on this fake BESTBall court was cheering. From up here, it looked like the best Bixonics promo ad ever staged.

"Now THAT is a commercial!" the director shouted.

Only Gray and Leo knew that that was hardly true.

"He underestimated you," Leo said in a hushed, rushed voice. "He won't do it again."

"Playtime is over." Felix Danvers appeared in the doorway to the court and back out again. Leo immediately wheeled after him, not even a goodbye. "Not to sound rude, but don't come back up here, Grayson," Felix called back. "We have serious work to do, and Leo doesn't have time for puppy love."

Gray's face burned. Leo wouldn't even look back at him.

And then? They were gone, and he was flanked by security on the long, long elevator ride back down to Earth.

LEO

4

Felix v. Leo

Leo was always searching for ways to escape.

They kept their hands busy, outsmarting their favorite video game with ease. This was the same game they used to play with Gray on the small couch in Box 242 for hours, elbows gleefully jabbing elbows. It wasn't as much fun with one player. Or with Sherlock. It was far too easy. Most things had become too easy . . . all except the things that were now impossible.

Like how to convince Felix to let them go down to ToP for Ace's trial with the program board. If Ace was kicked out of ToP because of his stunt on the roof, there'd be no aug for him after all. For most cadets, that would be a huge bummer. Leo knew Ace well enough to know— and their aug confirmed—that being kicked out augless would be too hard for him to take. Getting an aug was Ace's dream.

Leo kept staring at the clock like it had an answer inside the numbers. Only a few hours until some Bixonics cronies decided their boxmate's fate. Time itself was so weird up here. The last six months that Leo had spent under Felix Danver's tutelage had felt like a blip, but the three days since Gray had come to see them—and Ace had nearly died in the process—had felt like a few hundred years.

Of course Leo had easily worked out that Grayson was trying to rescue them when he offered to come shoot a commercial, but they'd never imagined that Ace would be put in harm's way in the process. Was the Resistance that desperate? Couldn't be. The movement seemed to be gaining ground from where Leo sat; Felix was so annoyed with the constant media coverage. Bixonics stock had even fallen for the first time since it had gone public. Cadets were being withdrawn from ToP by their families by the dozens.

People were so loud right now that Leo swore they could hear them even in space. But then, thanks to Sherlock, Leo knew the odds of the Resistance instigating an actual cultural reckoning on the empirical company. They weren't bad, truth be told. As long as Atlantis continued to spread truth and Dr. Bix was alive to keep Felix in check, there was hope.

But then, Leo couldn't help remembering Ace's plummet. He hadn't even looked afraid, the little hero. Just frustrated with his wings.

Oh, Gray. He'd looked *very* hurt.

Did he even get their message on the court?

And was Emma getting any of the secret twin language they'd been sending?

Being up here had somehow skewed their mental calculations. They were not on Earth but also not really in space. They were orbiting their home planet, but they weren't a part of it either. That felt like a metaphor for their brain as well. Inside their thoughts was the Sherlock aug, always decoding, deducing, cataloging, and predicting, but hovering at the edges was Leo, Lilliputian and BESTBall captain, Grayson's best friend and a key member of the Resistance.

It was a lot to hold in their head all at once, especially when most of their time was spent trying to fool the mad genius who *thought* they were playing along. Some days it seemed like he was onto them; other days, Felix's illness made him slightly easier to outmaneuver.

At least Leo hadn't made the mistake of trusting Felix. Or Bixonics. Not for a second. Not since the moment they'd woken up in that post-op room and realized that the entire training they'd undergone had clearly been brainwashing. Save the green puppy? Yeah, right.

Serve Bixonics or else was more like it.

The man named Felix had been waiting for them when they opened their eyes after aug surgery. He knew they

weren't tricked by the company's pretenses of wholesome-
ness. He was delighted that Leo was full of doubt, regret,
and anger. He was delighted that the Sherlock aug had
worked that well on their already powerful brain. He'd
whisked them away without another word, to "complete
their training" in space. For their "safety."

Leo hit pause on the game. Went into the bathroom.

They thought about Gray's bewildered, trusting
face—and got so mad they cried. Felix would be able to
tell, and he'd want to know why. Feelings and emotions
flustered him *a lot*. Quickly, quietly, Leo knocked their
elbow against the wall so hard it bruised. There, now they
had a reason for their red eyes.

When they came out of the bathroom, Mr. Danvers
was there, standing with his favorite Hercules security
guard, always his shadow. Danvers was never left alone,
and Leo was starting to understand that that might be
worth looking into . . . A weakness perhaps? Could they
be so lucky? What was he afraid of?

But that line of thinking would have to wait.

"You've been crying," he accused.

"Funny bone. Bad hit."

"Try again."

It was his favorite phrase and Leo's least favorite. It
meant that he wasn't buying what they were selling.
And he wanted Leo to try harder at deceiving him. He
enjoyed being able to see through someone as crafty as

Sherlock-augged Leo. No wonder Rosa had run to the Resistance and faked her own death. It was like being the string that the cat batted at and chewed on.

Leo would fake their own death too and head to Atlantis, if they could figure out how to do it without leading Felix straight to Jayla's family and the secret Resistance base. They wouldn't do that for anything. Which was why they didn't even try to run with Grayson the other day.

"I'm upset," Leo stated simply, truthfully.

"A better answer. Why?"

"My boxmate is going to be on trial this afternoon for what happened on the roof of ToP. I want to be there with him. He's important to me."

Felix squinted while unpacking that for more lies. He came up empty. Leo had already deduced that Felix had very few people that he cared about. They were starting to worry that having Sherlock meant losing connections with people in general. Even seeing Gray had been so . . . hard.

"Wouldn't you want to be there for your boxmate?" they dared.

"*My* boxmate. Ha!" Felix picked up the controller for Leo's video game. "My boxmate thinks he's invincible." He un-paused the game and within seconds, he'd won the level. Even Leo would have had to take a *few* minutes to crack it.

They narrowed their eyes on Felix. "You're smarter than me. I already know this. Why are you showing off?"

"Showing off? I'm simply reminding you who is the boss, but I'm not without kindness toward you, am I? I let your Grayson Bix up here, knowing full well he communicates with the Resistance. What a little rebel to his family!" He tossed the controller down. "And did you see his expression when I asked about his father? The man is clearly dying. I would guess it has already gone a bit far. A coma, even, if I'm lucky. Oh, I have been waiting for this information to reach me. Lance was so clever, hiding his condition and whereabouts from me. Creating that AI program to take his place. As if that would fool me."

Leo calculated whether kissing up to Felix or daring him would work better right now. They landed on something a little close to the bone, using the same trick Felix had used on Grayson back on him. "Did you ever care about your boxmates, Felix?"

Most people would have felt the sting in Leo's words. Felix felt nothing.

"Leo. I'm tired of this talk. I came in here to offer you something you want desperately."

Felix waited; so did Leo.

Time ticked by painfully slowly.

"Would you like to go down to the trial with me? My team of XConnects have created something exciting for me to try out. Although I'll need your . . . experience with a few things to sell it properly."

"Okay," Leo said too fast, and Felix chuckled and

moved toward the door.

"Be ready to go in half an hour." Felix paused. "Don't you want to know what I need from you in return? Or have you deduced it?"

"It doesn't matter what I deduce," Leo said. "You know I will trade anything to go."

He tapped his nose; they'd done well.

Once the door shut behind him, Leo's aug let them know in no uncertain terms that they'd just made a deal with a supervillain and the odds were not in their favor.

The deal was much worse than they thought.

Leo was in the Bixonics private jet—complete with bright green carpet—across from no one other than Dr. Lance Bix.

"Is this about the right pitch of voice, would you say?" the fake scientist asked.

"Yes."

"Elaborate, if you please." He wore a sharp brown suit and shirt with a green tie to match that carpet—and the facial expressions of a completely different person.

"If he were happily approving of someone or a situation, he would talk like that." Leo couldn't believe their words, but Felix was right; they'd agreed to do this without asking the terms.

Who was the fool now?

Dr. Bix twisted the knob on his wrist, and he became

Felix Danvers, grinning like the meanest kid who'd just gotten a new, more powerful tool. Leo often noted that Felix's maturity was behind. His jokes and way of talking, his sense of vengeance . . . He just wasn't a grownup.

Was it the aug or his personality? Who would know for sure?

Maybe his old boxmate: Coach Vaughn.

Leo felt a flutter of hope in their chest. This was hard, but they were also about to land on the roof of ToP. They would be there for Ace while this all went down. To be honest, the odds were not good for him, but maybe there was a chance for escape.

Leo wasn't sure, but they'd long since suspected that Dr. Bix hadn't built the space lab to keep Bixonium away from the general public, but to keep Felix away from everyone. They looked up at Dr. Bix, the newly wearable holograph.

This was bad.

"And what kind of voice does he use when he talks to his son these days? Like this?" he asked with a chummy sort of tone. "Or more like this?" He spoke more seriously. "I haven't seen them together since Gray was such a skinny little one, excited to take over his dad's company one day. That seems to have changed, by the way."

"Or was never true." Leo grimaced. It was bad enough that Felix had taken over the holographic AI software of Dr. Bix long ago. He'd been pretending to dial in as the scientist for some time at ToP and in board meetings . . . but now he was going to *wear* the holograph? Pretend to be Lance so that he could shake hands with the program board? Smile at the cameras in person?

Leo couldn't stomach the idea that he'd be pretending to be Dr. Bix to Dr. Bix's own son. He only hoped that Gray had decoded the message they'd burned into the court with their wheels. Felix had another motive that they'd deduced as well. He wanted to be out in public, but *not* as himself.

And that was perhaps information for the supervillain pile.

"You didn't answer." He scowled, and suddenly he did look an awful lot like disappointed Dr. Bix.

"He talks to his son more seriously. And also he's almost always rather deathly tired. Like you." It was a direct hit at Felix's soft spot, his own crumbling health.

Felix flicked back to himself. He stared out the window. "Well, you don't have to get mean. I'm not going to see or talk to Grayson. He won't show up for Ace today. He's too busy taking money out of his own trust fund by palling with the Resistance."

Leo wanted to believe that Gray was going to be there, and yet when they ran through the math in their head, they came up with the same deduction that Felix had. Gray was obviously not on Team Bixonics these days. They'd even heard grumblings from the board. He was stepping away from it all, hiding out in Atlantis with Jayla while Felix was stepping into Dr. Bix's literal life.

The jet landed vertically on a small circular landing pad that was specially reserved for this vehicle, Dr. Bix's famous personal jet. The media was waiting. Cameras hovered above the shoulders of newscasters and reporters. Leo rolled out, after the fake Dr. Bix.

Leo was shocked to be bombarded by questions and microphones. Flashes went off, and the jet engines made everything sound like they were screaming nonsense.

The security guards ushered them inside. The wind and chaos cut off as the door clapped shut behind them, muscled closed and locked by the guards. Leo stopped rolling to take a deep breath. The media banged and hollered on the door just behind them . . .

But, they were home.

ToP had its own unique smells, sounds . . . and light fixtures. The last one of these didn't feel right, though. Above, only one dim safety light was blinking. It wasn't like ToP to have any lights out. Unless someone had turned them out. On purpose. Turned the surveillance system off too, no doubt.

It was a trap.

Leo whirled in their chair seconds before Felix turned around as well. Standing in the shadow of the door they'd just rushed through was Coach Vaughn.

He looked to Leo first. "You all right?"

They nodded, relieved to see him. His face hardened with a supportive grin as his aug picked up those feelings easily.

Then he turned to the fake Dr. Bix. "Go back to space."

Felix sidled around Leo's chair to glare at Vaughn. "What are *you* doing here? You left ToP."

"I came back."

"You were fired!"

"It was forced leave. I did my time." Coach crossed his arms over his chest.

"Who let you come back? I'll fire them!"

"Not even you can fire the whole company board. Felix, stop this," Vaughn ordered firmly but carefully. Leo stared at their old coach. They'd never seen this side of him. He was nose-to-nose with his old boxmate, a brick wall of certainty and calm. "Leave the poor cadets alone. You don't need to be jealous or angry with anyone anymore. Karma already got Lance. I think it's on its way now for you too."

Felix looked too mad to speak, except he was still projecting Dr. Bix. Leo had never seen a look so ferocious on the good scientist's face. It looked wrong. "You don't know! You can't! You don't have feelings anymore. You only process other people's feelings."

"You know that's not true. Your aug is the only one that malfunctioned. I swore to you when we were boxmates that I would help. I haven't changed my mind."

Dr. Bix–shaped Felix sneered. "You're trying to give Leo information about me. Don't forget that I'm smarter than you. And I can have you banned from this building."

"Don't forget that there are many types of intelligence." Leo's old coach reached out and dropped a BESTBall in Leo's hand without taking his eyes off the enraged Felix. "Leo, the door."

Leo didn't think twice. They tossed the ball at the handle, popping the lock. They had to shoot back in their chair while the media poured in like a flood. The security detail that had retreated during the fight swooped in again and escorted Felix to the Coliseum.

Coach Vaughn vanished amid the chaos; it was the most apex thing they'd ever seen. And right before Leo's wheels, there was the path they'd been waiting for all year: a way to escape.

ACE

5

Ace v. Bixonics

Ace got dressed in his cadet shirt. He looked at his Bod and Brain track bracelets with pride. Then he gave himself his most serious face in the mirror.

"Not going to dress up? I'd wear a suit." Siff stood in his doorway, looking smug, or maybe he always looked like that. "If I wanted them to take me seriously, I'd dress seriously."

"I'm seriously a cadet. These clothes should remind them of that." Ace spoke like he'd already gotten kicked out. Everyone seemed to think it was a certainty. No one had faith. It was really starting to get to him. In Ace's mind, he had always flown off that ledge, no problem. He'd always landed safely, proving to everyone that he should have this aug . . . and also, stealing the world's spotlight so that Gray could get Leo back.

But there'd been no word from Gray or Leo or even Jayla.

In Ace's mind, he'd never once believed that this would fail or that the cost of this failure might be getting kicked out before he could get any aug, let alone his wings.

"You never think things all the way through." Siff sighed. "There are literally thousands of people here to watch this trial. Every bit of this is being streamed. *Should Bixonics be giving augs to twelve-year-olds who want to jump off skyscrapers? Tune in to find out!* I heard even Dr. Bix is coming to give a speech."

Ace knew Dr. Bix was frozen in Atlantis, and he wasn't going anywhere. But the holographic AI Dr. Bix? Yeah, it wasn't a great sign if "he" was coming. Ace could not even tell which side the holograph would swing, considering he had done something so unruly with a trial aug. "Go away, Siff."

"What? Why?"

"I don't need this right now. You're a bully." Ace had been getting better at having boundaries with his new boxmates, the ones who'd supplanted his beloved original crew. Maybe too good at it. At least Emma had graduated and was not in the box anymore, although Ace had seen her around, serving as grad aug. Leo's literal evil twin always felt like a spy. Or maybe that was just the nature of gossip media.

"You're the one who's shut off these days." Siff spoke calmly. "I've said I'm sorry for being so mean to you first semester. You don't get what it's like to be in constant nerve pain all the time. I had a reason for being a grumpy newb."

"Well, now I need a reason for your good humor. It's suspicious." Oh, wow, when Ace tried to sound like a grownup, he ended up quoting Mom. "Why do you bother explaining yourself? Do you think I'll just trust you? Like I'm that gullible?"

"Maybe it's not about you. Maybe I just got over being mean all the time." Siff was looking at his nails. "Leo got it. It's just . . . hard to be nice to you kids who are here for funsies. Leo's family made them come. They all wanted some fresh angle on Leo's disability. And me? I have a nerve disorder because my parents chose to genetically engineer my appearance and attributes, and oops, it sometimes causes bone-chilling nerve pain that comes and goes for no reason."

Ace had heard about biotech babies, although they were super rare . . . and always had mysterious genetic ailments.

"I needed NerveHack to save my own mind from being in pain. And you want to fly like a comic book character. We're very different people, Ace."

"See! You are still mean under all that. You think I'm stupid because I want to help people."

"How does having wings help anyone?"

Oh look, Ace's least favorite question. "See? You're still mean."

"Is everyone mean who second-guesses you? We have different perspectives and goals. And you can forgive me or not, but I will remind you again: Leo trusted me."

"*Trusts.* Leo *trusts* you. They're not dead. They're just . . . busy."

Siff sat on Ace's bed. Ace sat next to him. "I'm worried about Leo, actually."

"We all are." Ace could say more, but he didn't want to give Siff another shot. It reminded him of all the times he'd dared to believe that Finn could stop picking on him. But maybe—maybe—Siff could change. Maybe he already had, and Ace didn't even notice because he was too busy being hurt. "I'm sorry about your pain. That sounds awful. I did break both legs first semester. Oh yeah, you were there."

Siff frowned. "And how fast were you better?"

"In a few days."

"Yeah, that's not the same, but thanks to Dr. Bix and NerveHack, I can turn my overactive nerves off when they get too sensitive. I can play sports now and work on my homework without a migraine."

Ace had a flash of Siff sitting out of things in their first semester. Leaving class early. Scowling and snapping when people tried to talk to him. Ace wished he had iNsight all of a sudden, so he could begin to grasp what it might be like to be in that much permanent pain. "I don't think I *can* understand what it's like to be you, but I can try harder to forgive you for being a drudge first semester."

Siff laughed, but it was kind. "That's the most mature thing you've ever said, Ace Wells."

Ace squeezed his hands into fists over and over. "Thanks. I'll try to keep that in mind during my trial." It was time. Ace's heart pounded, and he was scared to be alone. What he wouldn't give for Jayla or Gray or Leo to be with him.

Instead, he had Siff.

"Walk to the Coliseum with me? I think it's time to get this done with. The being mad at you part. And some of the other stuff."

"It's too bad you can't show them how you can actually fly. That would give them something to think about before they boot you."

Siff walked him all the way there, and the strangest thing happened. It wasn't awful. Ace tried not to remember their first meeting in Otis. The way Ace couldn't stop imagining himself as a hero—and Siff as his archnemesis. Maybe his brother was right. Maybe he spent too much time thinking about things that weren't real.

The Coliseum wasn't set up with trial augs and stations— instead it had transformed into stands and an intimidating stage. Ace entered the familiar space with his heart thundering. The media and shouting people made it hard to hear himself think.

Siff gave him a squeeze on the shoulder and then went to sit with the other cadets. Ace headed toward the center of this uproarious spectacle. His parents were on the stage, sitting before a circle of chairs for the program board members. He stepped up behind their very familiar shapes in this incredibly intimidating arena.

"Hi, Moms."

His parents whirled around and swept him up in their arms. He was crushed in the middle of their love, and everyone could see, but whatever, he needed his moms right now. He'd never been so scared.

"You holding on, kid?" Mama Jay leaned over until they were eye-to-eye.

"No." Ace couldn't lie. "They're going to kick me out, aren't they?"

Mama Jay squeezed his shoulders. "We love you every which way."

And even that was a yes.

Mom hugged him again, and they took their seats in the center of everything. To the far left sat Finn. He didn't look over at his brother. He just stared ahead. Finn and Ace hadn't spoken since he'd caught his brother at the end of that plummeting fall. Finn had broken an arm doing it; it was already healed, but the rumors were that it was a bad break. Also, that Finn hadn't shed a tear while on camera. Emma had reported it all on her show; Ace knew that his brother preferred to cry when he was home, alone. He knew because their bedrooms shared a wall.

There was one more chair on this little accusatory island stage, and Ace nearly stood up and cheered when Coach Vaughn came over and sat beside him.

The arena grew silent as the program board filed in and took lofted seats around Ace's position in the middle. Legally, these things had to be open to the public, which was a weak spot that not even the Resistance had predicted. Now everyone knew that there was chaos at ToP, and everyone was watching to learn more.

Ace wondered if there were too many cameras rolling for the truth to get edited away. Too many voices calling out from the crowd, issuing chants for freedom from the Bixonics monopoly.

The head of the board stood and got everyone's attention. They were a somber, old one to boot. "Ace Wells is charged with stealing a trial aug, unlawful access to the rooftop, self-endangerment, and the endangerment of every single person who was absorbed by his stunt."

Oh, wow, they really were going to kick him out.

Mama Jay held his shoulder in support.

"Would you say you did all those things?" the board member finished lazily.

Ace couldn't find words.

In the silence, someone yelled, "*Resist Bixonics control! Run, Ace!*"

Ace snapped out of it; he wasn't going to run. He was going to fly.

He spoke into a hovering microphone. "I did do those things but I didn't understand . . . what I was doing . . . exactly."

"That's very clear," the primary board member agreed.

"I want to show you what I can do. Because I think it's more important than what I have done. And I did learn my lesson. I'm just lucky I had my big brother looking out for me." Ace had planned these words to highlight that Finn was one of their key aug stars, but that's not how it came out. "So, thank you, Finn. For saving me. Even though I wouldn't have fallen if you weren't there to push me in the first place."

Finn scoffed without looking him.

Mom whispered Ace's entire name under her breath.

These people had to believe in him. They had to *see* it!

"I need to show everyone something, before you make a decision about me."

Ace got up. He moved around the table. He jogged to where Siff sat with the cadets and whispered his hurried plan. Siff rolled out the tower that Ace used for training with the wings. Siff brought out a pair of trial wings as well, and Ace strapped into them.

Ace climbed the tower. He stood at the top. "How long has the SuperSoar aug been part of this program?"

his voice called out to the curious spectators and alarmed administrators.

The program board stared, and Ace had to repeat his question. When that didn't work, he answered it too. "Eleven years. And not a single cadet has been able to do this . . ."

Ace leaped off the platform. Hundreds of people inhaled sharply, but he flew. He glided in a circle, and then, he flapped. He was a bird. A natural.

He landed with a slight spring in the knees.

From the side, Siff whispered, "Superhero landing!"

Ace smiled and threw his arms up in victory. The crowd cheered.

Maybe they wouldn't kick him out.

He stood in the middle drinking their applause for a solid minute.

Coach Vaughn walked up with a slight tear in his eye. "You're going to have to trust me, cadet," he whispered.

"Course." Ace was confused. "Didn't you see? I flew so well!"

Coach put a hand on Ace's shoulder and hushed the audience. He snagged a hovering drone mic like it was a gym whistle and spoke into it. "And in eighteen years of teaching at this program, no cadet has ever broken that many rules and not been kicked out. Aug-less. People who don't follow the rules can become too powerful with an aug. We all know what happens. We saw it in that first class of cadets, my class. We've learned a lot since then. And I'll make sure nothing like that happens again. I'm sorry, Ace, but this should be a simple decision. Expulsion."

Now Ace was devastated.

"Coach?" he whispered.

Vaughn was turning all red beside him; Ace was so devastated that his feelings were ambushing the coach's iNsight aug. Ace was glad for it. He let his tears fall. He almost didn't notice that someone was walking toward their center stage public feelings duel.

Dr. Lance Bix's holographic AI walked straight at Ace, and he had to admit that this was the best holograph he'd ever seen. And then, the holograph stuck out a hand to shake. There was a new kind of stillness in the surrounding audience. Even when Dr. Bix was everywhere and healthy, he didn't come to campus that often.

But he was here? Now?

Ace shook Dr. Bix's hand.

The brilliant scientist was back; Jayla had saved him. Of course she had!

Ace was so relieved for Grayson, Jayla, the Resistance, everyone! "This is such good news! I'm so glad Jayla could unfreeze you!" And it had to be good news for this trial. This man could override any decision because he *was* Bixonics.

Dr. Bix's face flicked with a strange smile. "Me too."

He turned toward the school board and spoke loudly. "I believe Coach Vaughn is correct. Thank you, Ace, but it's time for you to go on to your next adventure." He flicked the mic away before he glared at Coach Vaughn and whispered, "Wouldn't want another Felix Danvers. Would we?"

The audience broke into loud reviews. Jeers, cheers, chants that picked up momentum. There was a shower of something soft being thrown from all over, and Ace looked down to find that cadets and alums were tossing their track bracelets onto the stage. One word became louder than the rest.

"Resist, resist, resist . . ."

Ace waited for the board's decision. He couldn't hear anything over the crowd being forced out of the arena by a sudden influx of Bixonics guards.

But then—as if he'd found the complete worst way to get noted on the arena surround screens—the streaming ads delivered the board's decision to him:

Ace Wells is expelled from the B.E.S.T. Program.

JAYLA

6

Antiserum v. Cure

Jayla was sitting on what could possibly be a cure for Bixonium poisoning.

She was also grounded, stuck on the couch in her undersea apartment. The plan to save Leo that she'd neatly concealed from her parents had backfired in so many creative ways. Ace had gotten expelled minutes ago, Gray still hadn't returned to Atlantis after his trip to Bixonics HQ, and Jayla had damaged the trust she'd been trying to build with her family.

Her legs were curled beneath her while she watched the livestream trial she'd hacked into with some serious parental convincing and Amir's network topside, transmitting the surface signal beneath the sea.

She could hardly believe that there was an actual riot happening at ToP—all because of Ace! She turned off the screen, unable to stomach how those Bixonics guards forcing people to leave campus were former cadets. Jayla tried to imagine what it would be like to have to use her aug to defend a company that didn't care if it harmed people . . . but she couldn't.

The screen in the wall blinked to glossy white, the chaotic sounds at ToP gone.

Jayla's mom came in with a bowl of cherries and sat beside her on the couch, concern creasing her brow. "Ace's parents will take him home now. He'll be in less danger now that he's out of that place."

Jayla wished she could believe that. Instead of responding, she ran the trial software wordlessly. Being grounded meant that she wasn't exhausted for once, and the result sprang up in only a minute.

[processing complete: antiserum compound successful, Bixonium degraded in virtual patient X]

Maybe she should have crowed and showed the result to her parents, but she couldn't. Nothing was ever this simple, and she needed to know more about the cost of this latest scientific breakthrough before she raised anyone's hopes too high.

Her mom didn't glance at her interface, but she did seem to always know what Jayla was working on. "Any luck with your formula?"

Here it was, a window to say *yes* and share her discovery.

"I don't know," Jayla said instead. "Why is it so hard to trust hope?"

Jayla's mom squeezed her foot. "We all believe in you. We're all wowed by your talents and flagrant disregard for the rules, but no one wants you to burn out before you can make a real difference."

"I'm not burned out," she muttered.

"You slept for nearly two days after we grounded you. I would call that burnout. It happens to your dad a lot, especially when he's on the verge of discovery."

Her interface buzzed, and she checked it.

[message from Amir: hey, grounded, just your daily reminder to talk to your parents about your world-changing, human-evolving discovery]

Amir had been nudging Jayla to tell someone about her formula breakthrough, but this wasn't the right moment. Plus she had to make sure it was a cure for Bixonium poisoning, not like a tincture to help it or something. Grayson had been through too much. When she told him that she was ready to dethaw his parents, she wanted to be positive that it worked.

The door to the apartment flew open and Jayla's dad swept into the room. He wasn't alone either. Gray was behind him, newly returned from the world above, as well as Stern and Rosa. They all looked really stressed-out.

Rosa was *upset*. She paced the living room, pulling at her hair.

"What's happening?" Jayla asked.

"Rescue," Rosa chirped. "You've got to go rescue his

whole family now. Now!" Jayla's dad held out a hand to calm Rosa. Stern tried to put some headphones over her ears to help her, and she batted them away. "You're taking too long!" they yelled. "Don't you know who's after them?"

"Who is after who?" Jayla's mom asked.

"Rosa has deduced that Bixonics will go after Ace for information about the Resistance." Jayla's dad's voice was low but sharp.

Jayla's mom was on her feet in a second. She crossed to the back of their apartment and came back with flight suits for both of Jayla's parents. They began to suit up.

"What's happening?" Jayla asked Gray directly. They definitely weren't going to let her come this time, and for whatever reason, that felt like something bad was certain to happen.

Gray's augged eyes were dark, tired. Where had he been the last three days? "Rosa was watching the trial topside, and when she saw that"—his teeth ground the next words—"*fake Dr. Bix* shake Ace's hand, she went wild with despair."

Stern kept a protective eye on his best friend and fellow Atlantis guard. "Rosa takes in information all the time. Sometimes it adds up to something rather certain that's about to play out. It's almost never good."

Rosa took Jayla's arms, speaking frenetically. "He knows that Dr. Bix isn't able to stop him right now. He's just . . . walking around in his place! He'll make his move and take as many answers as he can get from Ace. He wants to know where the Resistance base is. That poor kid won't stand a chance!"

"He?" Jayla asked. "Who is *he*?"

"Felix Danvers." Gray's voice was harsh as grinding rocks. "Leo got me a message when I was up there with them. Rosa has been helping me sort through it topside."

Rosa scowled. "*X* = *AI*. Hardly a nailbiter. *X* isn't for Bix, it's Felix. He always signed everything with an *X*. He thinks it's funny because that's shorthand for a signature. His sense of humor is . . . worse than Otis's."

Gray slumped on the couch. "We thought that the company's board hijacked the holographic AI that my dad left in control when he froze himself, but it's worse than that. Felix has been pretending *to be* my dad through the software. And apparently he can pretend to be my dad *in person* now. That's what made Rosa so upset."

"We're only safe when he's in space," Rosa sang under their breath.

Jayla's jaw nearly dropped. "Wait. The infamous unhinged Sherlock is heading Bixonics?"

"With Leo at his side," Gray added.

Jayla couldn't believe everything that was swirling around the living room. The space had been silent and cozy and home only a few minutes before. Her parents grabbed her arms warmly but firmly. They wrapped her in a hug that felt in no small part terrifying.

"We'll be back soon," her mom said.

"Don't worry," her dad added. "We're experts at getting in and getting out."

Rosa stood up. "I'm coming too."

Stern shook his head. "That's too much exposure for you. If Felix is there, he'll know you're still alive."

"You need me. I'm the only one who can predict what he's planning to do." Rosa was so certain that no one doubted them.

Gray moved like he was going to follow the adults and join the rescue, but Jayla's father shook his head. "We need you safe, Grayson. Stay with Jayla. If anything happens . . . well, we might need you to step up. We will protect you to the end, but also, you're the last card we have to play against Bixonics."

Rosa stared at Grayson. "You're bad for Felix's plans. Stay safe."

Jayla's parents left, followed by Rosa and Stern. The door clapped shut behind them, and Jayla and Grayson looked at each other in silence for a long, long moment.

"Poor Ace," Grayson finally said, collapsing on the couch.

"And Rosa. That Felix guy terrifies her."

"He should scare everyone. He knows too much, and he's oddly . . . childish? You know how everyone thinks my dad made that space lab to practice his work? I'm starting to think it was actually a place to keep his most dangerous failed experiment."

"Felix Danvers, the worst Sherlock."

Gray nodded. "I once heard Felix tell my dad that he would turn the cadets into an aug army . . . so, yeah, *unhinged*. I don't think Leo is on his side. Or maybe they are; they wouldn't even try to leave with me. I feel so stupid around them now. When I look at how Rosa has to live up in that guard shack with Stern . . . Will Leo ever be able to be around other people again? Or will they end up like Rosa and Felix? Brilliant and fragile?"

Jayla's mind snagged on something. "Why are you bad for Felix's plans, though? That was a pointed thing that Rosa said."

"Maybe because I understand Leo?" Gray asked hopefully. Then he shook his head. "It's probably because I'm next in line to head the company. If my dad were back, none of this would be a problem. He could just take over like usual and put Felix back in space . . . He could do . . . whatever he used to do with the company to make everyone happy and chill out."

Gray looked wild-eyed. "If anyone in the Resistance thinks *I* can do that in his stead, they really don't know me."

Jayla gave her boxmate a hug. He was right, if Dr. Bix were back, there'd be a lot fewer problems.

It was time to test her theory. She blew out a long, scary breath.

"I've discovered a compound that appears to degrade Bixonium, Gray." Jayla fought the fear living inside her words. "It might help your parents. But maybe not. I need to run some more tests. The equipment I need is in my dad's medical lab."

"Then let's go."

Gray and Jayla took the elevator down several levels, almost to the bottom where rows and rows of tenders sat in their little airlocks, an army ready for a large-scale emergency.

She shivered just thinking about it.

The elevator paused two floors above the seafloor, at her dad's most secret lab. Jayla's dad, Charlie, had several medical levels in Atlantis that he worked out of. Most of them felt like hospitals or doctors' offices. But not this level. This level was somber and cold, even before the elevator doors opened.

"It's waiting for a security clearance," she interpreted for Gray. She fired off a few commands on her interface, and the doors opened obediently.

"Are we going to get busted?" Gray asked tentatively. Then he shook his head. "Doesn't matter. If there's a chance this will work, we have to try. You heard them. All of our problems exist because my dad's not here to stop them. Ace is in trouble, and Leo is the right hand to disaster . . . We have to bring him back."

Jayla held out a calming hand. "This isn't necromancy.

He's not dead, and I don't know if we have what we need to save him yet. But let's see if we do."

They stepped into the cold, dark empty lab.

Jayla led them to the back by the twin chryo-tubes, the ones she visited every so often so that she could remind herself what was at stake. Jayla knew that Gray also came down here sometimes to visit his parents. She used her interface to remove the filter on the case, the one that hid their faces from view.

Gray and Jayla examined his frozen parents as if drinking in their determination. His parents looked so peaceful in their deep, medically preserved sleep.

Gray sniffed back some tears. "Do you think they dream?"

"My dad said it's more like disconnecting a computer from its power source. They're not 'on' but also the poisonous dose of Bixonium in their bodies can't cause any more damage." Jayla felt a revving in her heart, her pulse. She needed to solve this problem—and she knew she could. Her thoughts raced back to wherever her parents were, flying over the ocean, trying to get to Ace's family before the shadowy monster inside Bixonics got there first. Felix Danvers. The Sherlock skeleton in Bixonics's closet.

Jayla believed that her parents would succeed. They did these kinds of rescues all the time, and they always came back. Right?

Ace's family was as good as saved.

Right?

Jayla whirled into action. She turned on all the work lamps. The central floor was an open workspace. It surrounded a gurney that had a human shape beneath an ominous white sheet.

It looked like a dead body.

Gray came over and stared down at it. "What is that?"

"My dad calls it *HelperBot*. He invented it a long time ago. I was super afraid of it when I was a kid. Even had nightmares. He used to practice new aug surgeries on it, and now he uses it to test his treatments for aug-related health problems."

"I forgot that Charlie used to be one of my dad's lead aug surgeons." Gray took in the sheet, staring at the human-shaped head and torso, limbs, even the points of its two feet beneath the cloth. "So you're going to try your formula on it first? To make sure it works?"

"If the compound doesn't work, HB will tell us."

Jayla whipped off the sheet.

The medical dummy was solid white glass, just like the wall screen in her apartment. It had no features, just smooth shape. She turned it on with a flip of a switch at the back of its head, and the inside illuminated to show off organs, a nervous system, pulsing blood. Everything that was in the human body was represented in this dummy.

Gray was impressed. He used his VisionX eyes to scan it. "Wow. It's got all the stuff and blood . . . everything."

"Right? Pretty cool. Unless it starts chasing you in your nightmares, of course."

He smiled. "You can do this, Jayjay. I know you can."

Jayla nodded firmly and organized her thoughts. "It's really a two-step process. First, HB has to be identical to your dad's vitals. Which should be as easy as uploading his medical file into the hardware. Then we give the dummy a virtual dose of my compound and see how it reacts to the Bixonium in his cells."

The first step was actually very hard, but she eventually located where her dad kept Dr. Bix's medical file in his computer, uploading it into the software that personalized the internal makeup of HelperBot.

Gray and Jayla watched while the dummy took on Dr. Bix's unique physical inner workings, without losing any of its strange absent glass-ness.

"Okay. Now it matches your dad's blood type, organ sizes, metabolism, and . . . level of cellular degeneration." She whispered the last part.

Dr. Bix had been frozen in a secret way that had made it feel like he was going to be fine as soon as he woke up, but Jayla knew enough about her father's medicine to understand that the levels of poisoning she was looking at were highly toxic. If Dr. Bix hadn't been frozen, he probably would have died within days.

What was Dr. Bix doing with that much Bixonium inside him?

She kept this question to herself, and moved on to step two.

Jayla plugged her compound into the software that ran HB. It took a long time, and she was slightly aware of her interface sending her messages, trying to break her concentration. Most of them were from Amir. He was looking for her. She told herself she was too busy, and he would only distract her at this point.

She told her network to silence all notifications.

"Okay." She sat back, wiping sweat from her brow. Gray jumped up from where he'd been sitting at his parents' feet, looking up at them in their chryo-tubes. "I'm ready to try it. Are you ready?"

"Do it."

"I think this should work fast. I included a digital dye so we can see how it works. The Bixonium should show up as green, and the cure will be in blue."

"Your signature color." Gray grinned. She was glad they were doing this together. It felt right.

She entered the color treatment, and Dr. Bix's virtual HB body throbbed green in places all over the white-glass body. Next, Jayla injected the virtual compound into the dummy with a few light finger strokes on her interface.

When the elevator dinged, they both jumped. The doors opened and Amir stepped out, eyes sweeping the room for them. "Jayla, your parents are looking for you *everywhere*!"

"They're back from the rescue?" she asked. That was fast. Fast was a good sign. She blew out a huge breath.

Only, Amir's expression was too serious.

"What happened?" Gray snapped.

"You haven't gotten any of my messages?" Amir asked.

"I turned off notifications. What?" She tried not to yell, but it was like Amir *didn't* want to tell her something. "What is it?"

"They didn't get there in time to save Ace. He's gone. His moms too. No sign of his brother Finn either. Apparently Rosa had a complete meltdown and said the world was over, and Stern couldn't get another word out of her. She went catatonic."

Jayla was stunned. Ace's family was missing? Well, they weren't missing. They were in the hands of Felix Danvers. Which was so much worse.

Amir stopped talking, but the look on his face meant that he had more to say.

"What is it?"

"There's an emergency Resistance meeting happening right now. They're talking about evacuating Atlantis *tonight*. As soon as Ace reveals where we are . . . well, none of us will stand a chance."

"We need my dad," Gray said, turning back to HB. "Now."

The throbbing sections of green Bixonium poisoning in the dummy flared when the blue came in contact with them. The two colors struck a new balance, a kind of turquois swirl. The vortex of hope.

"Is that your cure compound?" Amir's tone was impressed, excited. "It's working!"

Jayla didn't respond. She was too busy watching every speck of green vanish within HelperBot's body. "It's only a cure if HelperBot survives. Otherwise it's just an antiserum, and Dr. Bix won't survive the degradation of the Bixonium."

She hadn't spoken her fear aloud yet. It had been gnawing at her for days.

"But it's going to work," Gray insisted. "I knew you could do it."

"We can't celebrate yet. We've got to get my dad on board and dethaw your dad. And if they're evacuating Atlantis, this could become a lot harder. Grab that end of the gurney. We're taking HB to the Resistance meeting."

All three of them rolled the medical bot into the elevator. The doors closed, and they began to rise.

Gray's VisionX eyes were gleaming. "I can't *wait* to see my dad stride into that stupid fancy space lab and take over the place. This is *our* company, and if Felix Danvers wants to play with it, he'll have to outsmart all of us first. And you know what? I don't think he's that smart at all."

Jayla smiled, laughed.

"What?"

"I've never heard you call it *your* company before."

Gray looked surprised too. "I don't think I ever have."

A warning sound started to go off on the bot. Jayla silenced it and then examined HB.

"What's happening?" Amir asked. "That didn't sound good."

Jayla checked the steadily plummeting vitals readout. "HB had a small heart attack. Probably shock from how effective the serum is." Her explanation was sound, although her tone had lost its pride. If she were her dad, she could do some kind of medical treatment for whatever was happening now, only she was not a doctor and so she could only watch while the dummy began to seize, organs failing.

By the time they reached the floor for the Resistance meeting, HelperBot's vitals had flatlined . . . and went out.

"*Antiserum*," Jayla cursed.

GRAYSON

7

Gray v. Hope

The Resistance meeting was full of shouting voices when Grayson Bix burst through the doors. No one even noticed when Jayla snuck in.

"We have no choice but to evacuate," Jayla's mom yelled, over the objections of many adults and former cadets in the room. "If Felix Danvers is aware of our home base, we have been assured that he will strike. Bixonics is as dangerous as the person in charge of it, and if the Resistance were to get control, Danver would lose his stolen empire. We can't let him take us out. We are the hope for the future." She softened, looking to her daughter. "Atlantis has been everyone's home for years, and we love it too, but we're sitting ducks in the ocean. The only safety we've ever had is in our secrecy. That might be gone now."

"We don't know that for sure!" someone yelled. "Maybe Danvers doesn't have Ace Wells or perhaps he's not as violent as we think!"

Jayla's mom held up a hand for quiet. "We went to Ace's family home, and it was abandoned. Rosa has deduced that the family was never even allowed to leave ToP after Ace's trial. They must be in Bixonics custody. We've trusted Rosa to guide us with their deductions for years now. They've always been honest, even when the truth was harsh. We would be fools not to follow their advice now."

"Wasting time!" Rosa snapped from where they sat slumped against Stern's shoulder. Gray had a flash of fear—the same kind that always happened when they were around Rosa these days. Was this Leo's fate as a fellow Sherlock? To know so many bad things before they happen that they can't even be around other people?

They can't even hope?

Is that what Leo meant when they said they were only safe in space?

"How do we know that Ace will give us away?" someone asked.

Gray nearly put a hand over his face. Not that he didn't trust Ace, but keeping things to himself was never the cadet's strong suit . . . and that's not factoring in an all-powerful Sherlock chasing after him.

"Bixonics wouldn't be stupid enough to attack a deep-scraper full of families!" someone else cried out. "Think of the bad publicity!"

Rosa stood up. "Attack? Who says attack? They'll save their army for land. The most likely course will be a seismic shock to the ocean floor that creates an underwater tsunami and wipes this entire structure out in a few minutes."

Now there was a very different kind of silence. A pained, fearful one.

"We do have a choice!" Grayson held the door open, beckoning Jayla and Amir to roll in the dummy. They froze in the doorway. Jayla's light of hope had gone out just like HelperBot's in the elevator, but that didn't mean that Gray had lost faith in her discovery. "Jayla has found a cure for Bixonium poisoning, and I want to try it on my dad. I want to unfreeze him. *Today*."

The room went from too loud to too quiet.

"You all know it's my decision." He'd never sounded more like his dad in tone and certainty. Gray flashed with pride and fear. "My dad left a video stating that it was my decision when to wake him. And I say it is today. With my dad back, the corporation will have no choice but to listen to him. He can save Atlantis, Ace, everyone."

The hardest part was that Grayson believed those words. And they were a lot heavier than all the words he'd ever said about *not* believing in him. His heart drummed against his chest.

"We cannot rush into something like that," Jayla's mom said kindly. "Even if Jayla made a discovery, it would take weeks to test a serum . . . before we could . . ." Her voice trailed off as Amir and Jayla rolled in the HelperBot the rest of the way.

Jayla shot a daring look at her mom. "Don't get too excited. I killed HelperBot, but before it died, all the Bixonium in its system *was* degraded in full."

"A successful failure? An antiserum?" Her dad's eyes were suddenly gleaming, delighted. "With Dr. Bix's vitals uploaded?"

Jayla grinned and nodded. Gray didn't know what a "successful failure" was but it made Charlie pick up his daughter and spin her around with excitement. He whooped.

Gray took advantage of the Resistance's pause. "We won't have to evacuate if my dad is here. He can go to the company. He can stop Felix Danvers from taking his place and corrupting everything!"

The crowd erupted again. Arguments shot all over the place.

It wasn't until Rosa stood up and crossed to the center of the room that everyone began to quiet again, watching the pained expression on their Sherlock's face. She turned her glare on Gray.

Gray was uneasy while she peered into his augged eyes, reading between the lines of his expression. Then she looked over at Jayla showing off her formula to her dad. He was still exclaiming quietly and immediately started tweaking something on HelperBot's hardware.

Rosa sighed. "If the good scientist returns to us, he'll be able to change the tide."

It was such a quiet prediction. Gray wasn't used to Rosa's tone. Usually the way they saw into the future was more certain and growly. "Will you pay whatever the cost, Grayson?" she asked him directly.

Gray thought about Leo. And Ace's family. "Of course."

She kept her eyes on his, her words aimed at the Resistance. "Raising Dr. Bix is now a better choice than evacuation."

With that, Rosa left the room. Stern followed.

And hope was rekindled.

Hours later, Gray was staring at the matching chryotubes. His parents were a few feet away and yet further than they'd ever been.

He put his hand on the glass, right over his dad's hand. "I know you trust me," he whispered. "How do I trust you?"

Jayla came toward him with light in her voice. "We're ready. My dad and I have cut the formula dose so that it absorbs more slowly. It should give my dad's medicines some time to heal the tissue damaged by the infection. Do you want him to explain it to you? He's really good at the doctor stuff. I know how scary this is."

"What about my mom?" Gray asked.

Charlie, Jayla's dad, stepped over. He wore his white coat and a serious but hopeful expression. "Gray, Lance left instructions that if we find a promising treatment for the condition, he's to be woken up first and treated first."

"So he can have it before her?" Gray yelled.

"So he can be the guinea pig." Charlie put a hand on Gray's shoulder. "Once he's dethawed, he won't survive a second freezing. This is our only shot. Our parachute. Once it's open, it's open."

Gray nodded, confused. "What if it doesn't work?"

He didn't need an answer to that. His dad would be gone forever, and Felix Danvers would still be coming for them.

"We want you to know the risks before you make this decision." Charlie folded his hands on his stomach. "Your dad has got so much Bixonium in him. He's mostly formula. We're going to do our best, but also you were not wrong in the meeting. We need him to dethrone Felix as soon as possible."

Gray wiped at a tear with his sleeve. "Why is there so much Bixonium in him? Why is my mom sick too?" He turned around. "I need to know the answer before I face either of them again."

Jayla had a few precise guesses; she only wished she were wrong.

Charlie looked at his daughter. "You're one of his best

friends. You can tell him."

"But I'm not sure—" Jayla started.

"You are," her dad finished, giving her a side hug. Grayson couldn't help but feel the cold emanating off his father's chryo-tube. He put a hand on the chilled metal.

Jayla was ready. "We think your dad was trying to give himself augs. We don't know when or how he did it, but his body is riddled with scar tissue. When the formula didn't graft correctly, he must have tried to take more to force his body to heal—but it only prolonged the rejection. Your mom was infected by being around him. He was radioactive with Bixonium. By the time he figured it out, it was a little late for her."

Gray couldn't help thinking about the divorce. The way his parents had simply stopped being in the same room together. And then stopped being in the same room as *him*. That was because of the poisoning?

So there was a reason his dad kept his distance, always communicating through holograph. Good thing their son could fix this; he had hope, faith, and a plan.

"I want to try. I believe in Jayla's formula."

Within minutes the medical level was transformed into a hospital room fit for a king. Dr. Bix's chryo-tube was wheeled into the center. Grayson watched from the wings while Charlie worked his medical wonders.

He didn't know when he fell asleep. His dreams were dark and chaotic. The ocean was making Atlantis sway and Ace was somewhere calling his name, yelling for help. Leo was there too, always wheeling twenty feet ahead. Even when he ran he couldn't catch up to them.

Gray woke to Jayla rubbing his arms, saying his name.

"Gray, come on. Come see."

Gray stood up, scrubbed the sleep from his eyes. He pushed the curtain out of the way and saw his dad, all laid out on a hospital bed. He looked too thin, still sick, and yet . . .

"Lance will need a little while to wake up, maybe days, but we wanted you to be here with him when he does," Jayla's dad said.

Gray put his hand on his father's arm. It was warm. And alive. "I'll be right here when he needs me. No matter what."

STEP TWO:

ASSEMBLE—

LEO

8

Leo + Bixonics

Leo was free.

Well, Leo was prowling through the air vents of ToP but after being held in space for so long, this did feel like freedom. They pulled themself through a tight turn, flashlight in their teeth. Silence was important; that and having Otis on their side, which was step one. They were on step two: find a new chair.

By Leo's significant mental calculations, they should be right over box 242 . . .

Leo turned another corner. They paused over the place where the slits let air and heat pass from chute to room. This was Grayson's old box. Leo used to hang out in here all the time. That wasn't exactly true; the two of them always hung out in Leo's room, which was generally cleaner and not full of Bixonics bribery gifts from Gray's dad.

Those presents were always such a slap.

All Gray ever wanted was to hang with his dad in person, but his dad hadn't been around for more than a flash visit in years. Leo paused. Their aug spun, folding together old information and new data. If both of Gray's parents had gotten Bixonium poisoning—his mom simply from being around his dad—of course they wouldn't have let young Gray be around them.

Otherwise he would have been poisoned too.

So, they were trying to protect him.

Leo tried not to get distracted, one of the real problems with the Sherlock aug. They decided to focus on scaring the hair off Siff's scalp instead. With a few twists of their universal tool, the vent swung open. They dropped down, hanging from their arms and then—*oof.* They landed in a puff of pillows on the foot of his bed.

Siff yelped, stood up, and spun around. His blond hair was tall and his eyes were covered by a sleep mask. "Who's there?"

"Siff, it's me," Leo growled.

Siff lifted off his eye mask. He had three night-lights in his room, each one a different brilliant color. It felt like sleeping next to holiday lights. "Leo? What are you doing?" He sat down on the edge of the bed, eyes huge. "There are *a lot* of people looking for you. They searched our box yesterday."

"The security detail has moved on to searching the

surrounding buildings forty-two minutes ago. I've been listening to their feed." They grinned. It really *was* fun to be able to see ahead of other people, though they had to try not to get impatient with others like Felix did.

Someone knocked on the door. Leo pulled the blanket over them and muttered, "It's your boxmate. You woke them up. Say you had a loud dream."

Siff answered the door and spoke to whichever boxmate had come to check on him. He sold his line beautifully, and then returned to his bed. This was why Leo had come to Siff. The boy was a born liar, though not a bad person, even if that kind of duality was tough for people like wholesome Ace to figure out.

Siff shut the door and lowered his voice to a whisper. "What's going on?"

"Bixonics is about to attack the Resistance. I had to get out and warn everyone, but they were tracking my chair. I abandoned it during the riot."

Leo had left the fancy green Bixonics chair in Otis, a message for the guards and Felix to puzzle over. They'd left a trail leaving the building and then doubled back to escape into the literal walls of ToP, a rather large mouse scurrying through with even larger plans. Leo had waited as long as they could, but it was time to move.

"I need a new chair. There are some chairs that fit me in the BESTBall locker room. I need your help getting in there. And I need a disguise."

Siff scowled. "I want to say yes. I want to help you, but . . . did you see how wild everything got after Ace's trial? People were threatening to burn the whole campus down. They had to be forcibly removed from ToP! We haven't even started classes again. They just want us to sit quietly and wait it out."

Leo knew the truth. They had to be so silent during their time in Bixonics HQ that it was hard to get the words out now. "Bixonics is worried about the cadets joining forces with the Resistance and turning against them. ToP is the company's flagship. They'll defend it more than the other company holdings. Our best chance for success is joining up all the cadets. This is where you come in."

Siff stared at his hands. "Me? Yeah, me and Nerve-Hack are such frightening tools against the Bixonics empire. Sure."

Leo leaned in. "I'm a frightening tool against their empire. And all I need is your help."

It took Leo and Siff an hour to sneak onto the BESTBall court, even with Otis getting them down to the right level.

Leo wore a disguise, but they also stopped every so often to avoid the sweep of the security lenses and the patrol of the administrators and grad augs that Leo had carefully memorized.

At least the Bixonics guards had moved along.

The campus felt on the verge of something big. Leo

knew Bixonics would most likely send all the cadets home soon; they couldn't risk everyone joining together.

Leo had Siff play lookout while they walked on their knees into the locker room. The place was dark, but so familiar. Full of such good, rich memories. The court they'd had in space only barely took out the sting of not being able to play with their friends again. And their coach.

Emotion came through their aug like a toxin that didn't make sense. At first they tried to solve the flood of feelings, and then they surrendered to the drowning sensation. They had to sit down in the dark on the bench and hold their head.

They nearly jumped a thousand miles when a hand touched their shoulder.

Leo looked up at Coach Vaughn. "How . . ."

"Did I surprise you?" He sat down next to them. "I used my aug. I can predict things more to the point of reality than you can. You know I've called each and every one of your games. I know the aug a cadet will choose from the moment I meet them. And I've been waiting for you to come here and get a new chair ever since I saw them hauling away your old one in Felix's stolen jet."

"iNsight can do all that?" Leo was stumped. "But Sherlock is the aug that . . ."

"Sherlock functions on logic. iNsight maps emotions. Guess what people use to make decisions more often than logic? Their feelings." Leo looked a bit stumped, so he continued. "Felix coming down here from space, risking exposure, wearing that Dr. Bix disguise, did that seem like a logical choice?"

Leo sat taller. "It . . . wasn't. I was so surprised when he wanted to do that."

"The most unfortunate part here is that Felix's feelings haven't changed much since we were boxmates. He's still driven by revenge. We don't know how or why, but his aug had a negative effect on his personality. I've spent a lot of time trying to figure that out. We've been worried it would take you over as well. Well, the rest of them were worried. I knew you'd see the light. You have the heart of a hero."

Vaughn got up and crossed the small locker room. He pulled a practice chair out, opened it, and locked the wheels in place. "I think I remember you liked this one."

Leo nodded and hopped onto the seat from the bench. They felt better, faster.

Ready.

Vaughn's tone was serious. "This place is a powder keg. The cadets need a leader right now, Leo. It's you."

"But I wasn't even a good BESTBall team captain. I don't know how to talk to people. Also, Sherlock and living with Felix has made that part so much worse."

Vaughn didn't even seem to register their complaints. Or were they excuses? "Gather your strength in secret.

Emma has been getting your messages, and it took a little prompting, but she's filming behind the scenes at ToP like you asked. Take Otis to sublevel twenty-seven. That should give you some space off the grid. I've done all I can. My role is, let's say crucial, but also my hands are tied. Oh, and Leo?"

They looked up, so relieved to have this moment together. "There's a present for you on the administration level. Something you need. I've given Otis permission to get you up there, but it'll take a crew to outmaneuver the guards."

"What kind of present?" Leo wasn't used to asking questions anymore. They always just seemed to know the answers, but Vaughn was right. Things could still surprise them—no, people could still surprise them.

"Oh, just something you can't live without. Let's call him . . . the spark of the Resistance. I bet he'd love that."

ACE

9

Ace + Finn

Ace was in a prison cell with Finn. So, like double prison.

Honestly, it was just an empty room on the administration level of ToP, but it felt like a jail cell in Ace's mind. Things were a bit bleak. After the trial had ended in a double whammy of being expelled *and* a whole riot happening throughout campus, Ace and his family had been escorted to this level for their "safety," or so the Bixonics guards had reassured them. But after several days of being locked in place, Ace had to call it like it was: Bixonics was treating them like they'd instigated the riot on purpose.

The guards seemed to be waiting on further instructions, but he couldn't tell what kind. Neither could Finn. Not that the two brothers talked very often. Finn still seemed ragingly angry with Ace, and at this point, Ace was pretty darn mad at him right back.

Ace sat on the little cot, knees folded up to his chest.

He tried not to think about how he was never going to get his aug. That seemed like a minor problem at this point, but for his heart, there was nothing minor about it.

Finn's TurboLegs were in reinforced rubber shackles after he'd tried to *zip* to freedom the first several times that the doors opened to bring them food. He sat on his own cot and tossed his legs up with a loud *thunk*. Sounded like his brother's legs were really heavy.

"How long do you think we'll have to wait?" Ace dared.

"It gets longer every time you ask."

Ace threw his pillow at his brother. "We need to work together, you bruiser!"

"We're in this mess because of you!" Finn shot him the dirtiest look of his life. "You're the one who's in love with augs, but also moonlighting with your Resistance pals. Didn't you think that would ever come back to bite you in the butt? Don't you think about other people ever? Our moms are locked up right now because of you."

"It isn't Ace's fault that Bixonics is an evil empire!" Mama Jay called out from where they were being held in the next room over. "And Ace is right. You two need to bury the hatchet, once and for all."

"You love each other," Mom added in a strong voice. "That's what you keep forgetting *and* why you're both so hurt."

Ace and Finn turned away from each other on their parallel cots. A long, long time clicked by. Ace surprised himself by not imagining his wings and freedom, but wishing that he had his iNsight trial aug. It might not have been the flashiest of aug choices, but Coach Vaughn was right, it suited him mentally as well as SuperSoar suited him physically.

Ace's voice finally came out with a growl. "If I had my iNsight aug, maybe I could figure out why you're so mean to me all the time. Why you always want me to fail. And call me Deuce even though you know it hurts my feelings."

"Ace . . . I'm just . . . jealous," Finn finally admitted. "And stop imagining yourself with augs. You really burned the bridge on that one. Be *real* for once. I can't talk to you when you're imagining superhero drudgery."

"Jealous?" Ace laughed. "How could you be jealous of me?"

"Because my legs are so fast that I've got a permanent job? I mean, in some ways, maybe I should thank you. This is the first time I've had a break from doing Bixonics promo since I graduated from the program." Finn sat up and glared at Ace. He rubbed his elbow, the same one he'd broken when he'd caught Ace after he plummeted off the rooftop of ToP.

Ace waited as long as he could. He softened his tone and even his shoulders. "Does it still hurt?"

"It feels weird. The whole thing exploded, you know. Into bone slivers. Only my leg bones have titanium reinforcement."

Ace winced. He should say that he was sorry, because he was, but those feelings were better at staying on the shelves these days. When he tried to get one down, they all fell on his head. "And *you* say I'm too skinny," he tried to joke. "Imagine if I weighed as much as I should. I would've crushed you."

Finn looked like he might say something nice. Maybe something to help patch the open wound in Ace's chest. He'd spent the last year lying in bed and debating: iNsight or SuperSoar, which aug would he choose?

Now it was such a different debate: no aug or no aug?

Ace wished he had his Otis walkie. Or that Dr. Bix would come back and release them. Certainly Grayson wouldn't let the company keep them captive like this for too long? Maybe the Resistance was doing something, and this was how they were keeping him safe? Was that a silly thing to believe?

The door unlocked, and they both jumped to their feet.

The holograph of Dr. Lance Bix walked into the room, and without even thinking, Ace took off his shoe and threw it. It passed straight through the 3D image this time. So this was the holograph that he shouldn't trust; not the good scientist who'd come to his trial and shook his hand.

Where was *that* Dr. Bix now? Putting out Bixonics

fires? When was he going to let them out? Maybe the riot had spread. Maybe the entire company was in jeopardy. Ace didn't even know what that could mean. He hoped everyone in Atlantis was safe.

"Finn and Ace, two of my favorites," the Bixonics hologram said.

"Who are you?" Finn asked in a sharp voice, surprising Ace. "I know you're not Dr. Bix. I know you're not even the AI he programmed to take his place when he got sick. I'm not stupid."

Ace was surprised by how bold his brother was in this moment.

And by how much he knew.

"That's rather clever of you, Finn. No, I'm not Dr. Bix, and to be honest, I'm a little tired of wearing his image." Something flicked, and they were staring at a brown-haired, skinny man.

Finn just stared.

His hair might be streaked with silver now, but Ace knew who he was from all the research he'd done on Sherlock for Leo two semesters ago.

"Felix Danvers?!"

"The one and only," Felix replied. "The assigned villain, though only when you don't see things from my side."

"You're supposed to be dead," Finn whispered.

"Not dead. Just shut up in space. Speaking of, I don't believe your family is very comfortable here, so I'm going to make a deal with you. You tell me where the Resistance base is and your whole family gets to leave, with a sizable check from the company, might I add."

Finn glanced at his brother. "Don't say anything."

"I would never tell him, and also, he'd never find where they're hidden! They have security measures you can't even imagine. And numbers! They have Dr. Bix!"

And that right there delighted Felix in a way that sent shivers through Ace. What had he just admitted? Why couldn't he stop talking when he needed to?

Finn moved to his brother and put an arm around his shoulders. "Stop talking. He can deduce things you aren't saying, remember?"

Ace sealed his lips, but Felix seemed done with them. He turned.

Finn shouted, "You said you'd let us out!"

"I'm not often truthful, though. It's what makes people call me evil." He left, but not before Ace saw the gleam of victory in his eye.

Finn took in Ace's face. "You're so naive! I don't know what to do with you. It's like you think everyone is *good*."

"You think everyone is evil!"

"Everyone is looking out for themself, Ace. And that *is* a kind of evil. You want to know what it's like to have the fastest legs in the world? To be one of your superheroes? I know a thousand different ways that people want me to help, but do they ever ask what I need? Nope. Never."

The lights went out.

The room was very black. Ace heard his moms call out in worry.

Ace's voice came out small. "This doesn't feel right."

A voice floated down from the ceiling, slipping through the dark. "What do you need, Finnegan Wells?"

Ace knew that voice, but why couldn't he place it? Maybe because his heart was a screaming riot in his chest.

Ace's brother kept a firm grip on Ace's shoulder. "Who are you? What are you doing? What do you want?"

"My question first. We don't know if we can trust you, Finn."

Finn was silent. Ace felt like iNsight was inside him, all of a sudden. He felt it nudging him toward empathy, toward understanding.

"My brother needs a break," Ace answered. "He needs to be free."

Ace's brother squeezed his shoulder. Was Finn . . . agreeing?

The sound of a vent opening and someone dropping through made the brothers whip around in the dark.

Leo clicked on a flashlight.

"Leo!" Ace exclaimed, hugging them.

Leo grabbed Ace's arms. "The power surge will only last for a few minutes. We have to move faster than fast. But first, I need to know if you trust Finn. We can't take him if he's a Bixonics informant."

"Can't your aug tell?" Ace asked.

Leo's smirk had a tiny bit of whimsy. "I might have recently learned that my aug has an enormous flaw. And it's the fact that humans are driven by emotions, not logic."

By the light of the tiny flashlight, Ace looked at Finn. His brother looked angry, tired, weary to the bone. "We can trust him. And he trusts Dr. Bix. The real Dr. Bix."

The door unlocked and opened. Ace and Finn were rushed by their moms. Behind them, instead of Bixonics guards, Siff and half of the BESTBall team were wearing black and sporting all kinds of trial augs as spy gear. Even Emma was there, camera rolling and waving a silent hello behind it. Leo looked at her exasperatedly.

"What? We need documentation of everything happening in here," Emma said. "You said that, not me."

"Fine, but we need to *move*." Leo looked at Ace kindly but seriously. "I love you, Ace, but I just heard you give Felix the clues he needs to find Atlantis. We have to get a message to Jayla before it's too late."

JAYLA

10

Jayla + Parents

Jayla checked in on Dr. Bix in his hospital bed. He hadn't technically woken up, but he'd had so much brain activity in the last twenty-four hours. Everyone felt hopeful, despite the threat level in the deepscraper being raised to orange.

Throughout Atlantis, the lights had a reddish tinge, reminding them all to be prepared to leave at any moment.

Gray was asleep in the chair beside his dad. She put a blanket on him, and he stirred. "Any change?"

"Any minute now." Jayla believed it too.

Grayson still looked worried. He stared at the orange warning lights overhead. His dad's condition, while improving, was still critical. Jayla's antiserum degraded the Bixonium steadily, slowly, while Jayla's dad's medicines worked hard to regenerate lost tissue and vital circulation.

"He's getting better, Gray. And also . . ." She pulled up a chair. "My dad and I have been talking about his condition.

He kept away from you because he was literally radioactive with Bixonium. It seeped into the people around him."

"Felix Danvers has Bixonium poisoning too. I probably should have told you that, although he didn't seem as bad off as either of my parents. He was my dad's assistant in space." Gray crinkled his brow. "Wait, do you need to check my blood for contamination?"

Jayla smiled at him as big as she could. "No. If you had anything strange in you, they would have found it during your aug surgery. But we can test to be careful."

Gray held out his hand, and Jayla used her dad's on-the-spot microscope to examine a prick of blood on Gray's finger. "Look at that. Healthy. Turns out your parents did protect you."

"He could have told me the truth." Gray glanced at his dad's sleeping face. He kept thinking of Felix wearing his father's image. It horrified him deep down. "What about Leo? Do you think we should check them for Bixonium poisoning? They've been in space with him for months."

Jayla nodded. "We will as soon as we can. The good news is that even if they are sick, we have a treatment now. There's hope." They were silent for long minutes, nothing but the beep of the machines around them.

"So . . . where's Amir?" Gray asked.

"How should I know?"

"Because you're inseparable."

"It's not like that. Not exactly?" Jayla planted her feet.

"I don't know what's happening between us." It was a relief to open up to Gray.

"Have you kissed?"

"We have not . . . yet."

"But isn't it like kissing when you link your networks together?" Gray joked—and got swatted for his humor.

Jayla blushed, smiling larger than she had in years. "Atlantis is buzzing right now. The world that your dad is waking up to has gotten stronger, and they're all blasting countermedia. Even Rosa said that Atlantis is like the Resistance's flagship now. We're the heart of this. When your dad's better, we won't have to worry about Felix. We could . . . take a vacation! Can you feel it?"

"I can feel it." Gray liked hopeful Jayla. "And I can feel you finding your place in medicine." He tapped the sleeve of her white coat.

She twirled with joy. "I'm so glad someone noticed."

"Everyone noticed. You're going to become a doctor, aren't you?"

Jayla gave him a dismissive, yet beaming, look. She felt so happy, and yet when her mom came to the level where Jayla often worked side-by-side with her dad, Jayla immediately thought something was wrong.

"What happened?" she barked. It always felt like the rug was about to be pulled out from beneath the boxmates.

"Something serious," her mom replied. "Your father is going to meet us there. Come on. This is important." Her mom turned around and stepped back into the elevator and Jayla followed, knowing that they were most likely off to the level where they held emergency Resistance meetings. Or evacuations.

Jayla was quiet next to her mom. At one point, her mom looked over with a serious eye . . . but was that a bit of mischief in her expression? Jayla didn't even notice that they'd sailed by the level she thought they were going to.

When the elevator doors opened up at the central food court—and Amir and her dad were standing there with an ice cream sundae in each hand—her jaw dropped.

"What's happening?" she asked.

"It's your birthday." Her mom squeezed her from the side.

"Not until next week."

Amir shook his head. "Jayla, Jayla. You set calendar alarms for everything now, and honestly? You forgot to set one for your own birthday."

"Happy birthday, baby girl!" her dad crowed and gave her a hug. "Hero of the Resistance, and now fifteen years old!"

Jayla blushed and took the ice cream that Amir was holding out to her. "I got you chocolate on chocolate. That seemed like the safest choice."

"Incorrect," Jayla said, already digging in. "It's the correct choice."

The four of them found a spot beneath the huge tree of Atlantis—the one that had inspired the secret logo once upon a time. They ate ice cream together, laughing at jokes. Anyone who walked by might just think they were a regular family.

At one point, her mom referred to Amir as her *boyfriend*, and then Amir and Jayla looked at each other—they were going to have to talk about that later. She was surprised to be excited about talking to Amir. She wanted him to be her boyfriend, which was a cool and steadying feeling.

Jayla ate all the ice cream. She glanced at her network, and, yeah, it really was her birthday. "I think I need to work on my work/life balance."

Jayla's parents laughed together, warmly. "What if," her dad started, "you let us take over from here? You go to school. Hang out with Amir. Maybe join the swim team or something. A job in the Resistance is always going to be waiting for you."

Jayla giggled. "Is being a revolutionary 'a job'?"

Her mom's eyes were near sparkling as she took in Jayla proudly. "We're not going to be 'the Resistance' much longer. Your formula . . . what you discovered . . . Jayla, do you know what it can do?"

Jayla had recognized one of its rather stunning applications. She'd just assumed no one else had. "You mean as a de-augger?"

Her mom lit up. "We can open a business to rival Bixonics. We have the means to take offending augs out of people's lives!"

Jayla pushed her empty bowl away. "I imagine you're going to want me to get rid of my aug."

"No," her parents said at the same time.

Now, that was surprising.

"You don't?" she asked.

Her mom took a deep breath. She composed herself and spoke as if she were readying to admit something huge. "Your aug is . . . good for you. I can allow that. I can see that you don't have an aug that ruins your life like Rosa, and some of the others. You've worked so hard to make it your own. I'm proud of my . . . augmented teen."

Her mom's words had felt so necessary, and yet they'd also felt so heavy.

"Okay, but what if we don't go straight to de-augging people with my formula? What if we give them the aug they always wanted?" Jayla looked to Amir for support. He nodded encouragingly.

"Think about Amir and me. We both had to retrofit our aug so that it was what we wanted and not what Bixonics wanted to give us. We were lucky that we had the power and knowhow to do it. We should make this possible for a new generation of cadets. Think about it. They won't have to order off the fast-food menu at ToP for their aug selection. They could augment their bodies and minds however they wanted to. However they needed to. No more tracks or career paths assigned by aug choice."

Jayla's mom sat back, a bit stunned.

Her dad chuckled. "Your brain, my daughter, is a thrilling landscape. I do believe you just blew your mom's idea out of the water."

Amir nodded. "If you think about it, Jayla's current formula is a big step in the right direction. I have no doubt that if we all put our heads together, we could have a revised Bixonium formula that doesn't cause poisoning, and also might even allow for people to have multiple augs or hybrid versions of augs."

Jayla felt the fire in her belly that had sent her running off to ToP in the first place, against her parents' wishes. Her stubbornness hadn't gone anywhere, but at least her maturity had grown to match it. "I see that you don't want Bixonics to exist. Or augs or ToP or any of this global chaos. But it won't go away just because you don't want it around. Technology pushes forward. We move with it and grow, or we don't. Even this place we're sitting in couldn't exist without amazing, advanced technology."

Her mom reached across the table and took Jayla's hand. "I believe you, Jayla. You've changed my mind about so much of this already."

"And that's harder than discovering a cure for Bixonium poisoning." Her dad laughed. Jayla's mom swatted at him playfully, and then they were all laughing.

Like a happy family. Again.

Jayla took a picture with her network—but then a blast of sound deafened her while Atlantis shuddered top to tail, over and over. The windows around the tree of the Resistance cracked. Water began to trickle in, one drop at a time.

A robotic emergency voice came over the loudspeaker: *"Evacuate. Evacuate. Massive seismic reading. Calmly make your way to the top or bottom level, whichever is closer. Evacuate. Evacuate. Underwater tsunami headed our way. Estimated damage will destroy structural integrity."*

Jayla and her family sprinted for the elevator, where dozens of people were trying to cram on. "I need to get Gray and Dr. Bix!" she shouted over the fearful masses. She sprinted to the stairs, and her mom only barely caught her shoulder, pulling her out of the stream of people headed down for the emergency tenders.

"Jayla, you have to go down, not up. Your dad and I will get them, trust us."

"I'm not leaving them!"

"No," her mom said, giving her a huge hug. "You're going to save Gray's mom. You and Amir. Get her chryo-tube in a tender and get out of here! We'll meet you on the surface."

Jayla and Amir held hands as they rushed through the medical level with the chryo-tubes.

Icy water was already pouring in from the ceiling

vents, and some of the lights were flickering. They were both wet up to the ankles.

Estimated time until impact: one minute, forty seconds.

"Where is she?" Amir called out over the sound of the alarms.

"This way!" Jayla wove through the medical equipment, trying not to think about her parents going to Dr. Bix, no doubt. It would take both of them everything they had to get his hospital bed topside and in the helo on time.

But they would do it.

They had to.

Jayla found the tube with Grayson's mom inside. Amir engaged the hover function, and they tipped it into the water, now over their knees. It bobbed to the surface, buoyant. They took turns pushing it like a log down a river, all the way to the stairs.

When they got the door open, the tube shot down the stairs along with the rushing water, and Amir and Jayla had to chase it. They tripped down the waterfall of the stairs, all the way to the bottom and found that there were only three tenders left.

The first two they tried didn't work. They seemed to have been left because they were faulty. Which did not bode well for the third one.

Estimated time until impact: forty seconds.

They pushed the chryo-tube into the last option and

climbed in. Amir revved the engine a little hard, but this time it *did* turn on.

He blew out a terrified breath, readied his hands on the controls. The air lock opened and they shot free of the structure. Amir spun the tender so it was facing away from Atlantis, and set the engines at full speed. Within seconds, the wave reached the deepscraper.

Sound was magnified in water; Jayla always forgot that.

She'd never forget it again. The sound of Atlantis being beaten by water filled the ocean like a hundred nuclear bombs.

The tender spun horribly in the wake. Jayla and Amir screamed, gripping their harnesses and thankful for the foam of the headrests. When the tender finally stopped, the windshield had a huge crack in it.

Jayla stared at it. "Amir?"

"I see it." He took the controls carefully and set them toward the surface. With each passing moment, the glass fractured a little more, a little more.

"Are we going to die?" Jayla gasped.

"I really hope not."

"I really like you. Just in case you don't know. Now you do."

"I really like you too."

A second huge fracture started to let in fine sprits of water. Jayla could see the blue of the sky beyond the surface. They were depressurizing as fast as they could.

The windshield was more cracks than glass now.

Jayla couldn't stop from flinching. And right then?

They broke through the surface.

GRAYSON

11

Gray + Dad

Gray was asleep with his head leaning on the side of his dad's hospital bed when the evacuation alarm sounded.

He jerked awake, but he didn't move. Someone had to be coming to help him with his dad, and he wasn't leaving his dad behind for anything.

Not even a tsunami could make him.

Jayla's parents, Charlie and Aria, swept into the room minutes later, grabbing equipment. They sealed Gray's dad in a medical pod, and Gray squished in behind them in the elevator. The security system fired off another warning, but he could barely hear it over the roaring of the ocean around them.

Dr. Charlie pressed the button for the top floor, and Gray was surprised.

"We're not going to take a tender out? Isn't that easier to hide from Bixonics?"

"We're not hiding anymore. Not with him," Aria said, patting the top of Dr. Bix's pod. "Besides, it's a little too late. Bixonics did this. They know where we are."

"Bixonics couldn't do this!" Gray said, and then, "How could they cause a tsunami?"

Charlie sighed. "I wish they couldn't, but the company has powerful technology. The aug program is one small part of their empire. They do a lot of seafloor mining. And yeah . . . they know how to cause a tsunami with a few well-placed explosives. Rosa has been suspecting an attack might come that way."

Gray was shocked. This was his dad's company. His dad's legacy.

Which made it Gray's legacy too.

And for the first time he *really* wanted to do something about it.

The elevator was rising slowly, depressurizing slowly. Gray was sweating so hard the back of his shirt was sticking to him. "How much longer will this take?"

His words were cut off as the central security system issued another garbled warning. This one was a countdown. *Nine, eight, seven.*

It felt like time was being drawn out like a piece of taffy.

Five, four, three, two . . .

The tsunami hit the deepscraper like an axe. Everything went sideways and too fast. They all crushed each other, and in the aftermath, Gray was stunned that they were only mildly hurt.

Although his dad was no longer asleep.

Dr. Bix's eyes were open, and they were dark with fear. Gray put a hand on the clear lid of the medical pod. He tried to tell his dad with his expression that it was okay.

Even though it wasn't.

"Should we open it?" Gray shouted.

"He's safer in there than we are out here," Charlie shouted back.

The emergency lights flickered, a light blue color that made everything look like an aquarium. Charlie and Aria started whispering, arguing about what to do. None of the controls in the elevator were responding, no matter how many times the adults jabbed at them.

Water burst at them from all angles. Gray clung to the pod with his dad in it. He had no idea what to do. Aria yelled "elevator" into a small handheld communication device, and he thought he heard Stern, but all Gray could hear over the spray of highly pressurized water was the pounding of his own heart.

"Help is coming!" she said. "Hold on!"

The water was so cold that Gray began to quiver and grow numb. Charlie was shaking him for a few seconds before Gray even realized it.

"Can you see Stern?" Charlie shouted.

Gray blinked a pattern, activating the part of his eyes

that could see through walls and water. He saw heat waves and cold zones. There were a few more people trapped on levels above them. But mostly, he saw a massive, red-hot person coming toward them through the ceiling like a spider descending from its web.

"Stern," Gray croaked, pointing to the ceiling of the elevator. "Incoming!"

Charlie scurried on top of the medical pod and pushed open the trapdoor in the roof.

"Hello, let's go!" shouted Stern.

He grabbed the top of the elevator and latched it to his belt with a big chain. Then he started to climb, lifting the elevator with him.

Even for Stern, it was hard. He was sweating through his clothes, his eyes bloodshot. When they made it to the top, he lifted the entire elevator out of its chute and set it down beside the guard shack.

Rosa was waiting with the helo engine running.

Charlie and Aria ran to load Dr. Bix's medical pod into the helo, and Gray looked at Stern. "There are fourteen more people down there. Three are two levels below the surface and the rest are on sublevel fourteen."

Stern nodded and crawled back down the chute. Gray watched him go, wishing he could do something. Charlie came running back to him, grabbing his arm.

"We've got to get airborne! We've got to get out of here before Bixonics comes by searching for survivors!"

Gray nodded, but he still felt drawn back to helping Stern save those people.

"Come on, Gray! Your dad needs you!"

With that, Gray shot back toward the helo. A tender with a fractured windshield crashed onto the platform beside them. Jayla jumped out and hugged her dad. Amir opened the back of the tender, and Gray followed him, getting a hold of the chryo-tube containing his mom. He helped push it toward the helo and helped everyone inside.

He jumped in last and was still strapping in when Rosa launched the vehicle into the sky. His dad had gone unconscious again, and Charlie was monitoring his vitals inside the pod.

Aria was busy sending out signals to the tenders and other survivors of the attack. "I think most of us made it out. Stern is looking for the rest, before . . ."

"Before what?" Gray asked, voice cracking.

"The entire structure will lose its anchor with the seafloor. When it floods, it will . . ."

"Shipwreck," Gray finished.

Aria held her daughter's shoulders in the slowly circling helo. Her voice came out with the slightest tremble. "Can you see survivors?"

The word kicked his brain into action. He used his augs to check the water below them for tenders. The sea was full of them, and they all seemed to be all right. The evacuation had been successful. "Hundreds of people. No, thousands."

Before Gray could breathe a little easier, he heard a spine-snapping crunch. He turned, looked down. The center point of the guard shack of Atlantis broke, and fell into the sea.

The rest of it started sinking. *Fast.*

The water stormed with enormous waves of air escaping from so deep that they ruptured the choppy surface. Within seconds, any sign of Atlantis was gone.

"Grayson, you see my buddy?" Rosa called back.

Gray didn't.

He searched the water with his augged eyes.

And searched. And finally . . .

"Stern!" Gray pointed. "He's got a few people with him. Over there!"

Rosa powered the helo across the water. The small group that Stern had saved were drenched and frightened. They huddled in while Rosa left her pilot's seat to pull Stern out of the water, though he was so big she could barely move him. He was so tired he could barely move himself.

When Rosa had managed to roll him in, she climbed on top of him and hugged him like he'd saved her too.

"Where do we go now?" someone asked in a shaking voice. "Bixonics is surely coming for us. They'll say they're taking us somewhere to help us, but then they'll split us up."

Aria looked to Rosa. "Where would be safest?"

Rosa fussed with the controls. Shook their head. "I'm not seeing good options for us. Atlantis was our home base. That's why he attacked it. We'll be scattered now, less effective. Demoralized."

Gray stared at his father, still medically asleep. They needed someplace where they could care for him. He needed the best care, and then he would take care of Felix Danvers and his stranglehold on their family's legacy.

Rosa sent out a distress call. Amir and Jayla did as well with their networks.

"He took our flagship," Gray said. "So we should take his. We go to the Tower of Power. We make a last stand."

Aria looked at Gray with rising concern. "Gray . . . that would be like going into the lion's den."

"Yeah, but it's our den." He found Jayla's eyes. She agreed with him. It was all he needed. "Tell all the survivors to go to ToP. With half the students withdrawn, there's plenty of room. It's going to be our new base, whether Felix likes it or not. From there, we can strike out with strength *and* visibility. Jayla, call Otis and tell it to leave the door open."

Jayla entered a few commands on her interface. Then she looked up at Gray, her expression full of shock. "Ummm, you need to hear this." She pressed the speaker that allowed others to hear what she heard directly in her head.

At first, it was just static.

"Otis?" Gray yelled. "Otis, no time for jokes. Are you there?"

"Rather risky telling Otis *not* to joke," Leo replied.

"Leo? You're at ToP?" Gray was washed with relief, and then confusion. "Are you . . . with Felix?"

"No, they're with me! I'm here too! Leo rescued my whole family!" Ace yelled, making the connection crackle with the strength of his voice's volume.

"I'm okay. I escaped from Felix . . . and I know what happened to Atlantis," Leo said quietly as if they were talking directly to Gray. "I could see it, but I couldn't stop it. But we've got ToP ready for you."

"You've 'got ToP'?" Aria cut in. "What does that mean?"

"We took it over. Kicked out all the Bixonics employees," Leo said matter-of-factly.

"Cadets are in charge now!" Ace's voice sang out. "And they're all on the Resistance side! Well, most of them. Coach Vaughn is iNsight hunting for spies."

Gray laughed so hard it felt strange. His whole body felt like it was vibrating with power, with irrepressible hope. "You heard them, Rosa. We go to ToP. Tell the others to meet us there."

"Yes, sir," Rosa said, and it took Gray a long while to realize that he'd taken charge of the Resistance without even realizing it.

It felt right.

STEP THREE:

win—

LEO

12

Leo & Gray

Leo sat in the dimly lit hallway of the roof access. This was where they first saw Coach Vaughn *really* use his aug—and on Felix. It was a little intimidating to be back here facing Vaughn now, discussing how they were about to have a Resistance helo landing on top of the Tower of Power in broad daylight.

Coach Vaughn acted like he wasn't an emotional super genius, though. He hung back and nudged Leo along as captain. Siff, Ace, and Emma were drinking in their assignments like Leo was their favorite professor, listening to their every word.

"We make sure Dr. Bix is seen when we unload. We make sure that the story everyone knows includes him being back *and* sick, right, Emma?"

Leo's twin nodded.

"This will hold Felix back, hopefully long enough that

we can untangle the company board from his control. Felix, at least, won't be able to holograph in as Dr. Bix if everyone thinks that Dr. Bix is in the hospital at ToP." Leo took a deep breath. They were still getting used to using their voice so much. In space, their deductions were only ever sketched out with Felix. He could fill in the rest. This group needed a presentation.

"Felines?" Leo said, turning to the six cadets with FelineFinesse augs and strong, swinging tails. "Your jobs are the camera drones. We want Emma's feed to be the one that everyone has to watch. It'll be the only one not running through Bixonics's company filters."

They looked back to Siff. "You're filming for Emma. You got this. Don't flinch. Well, with NerveHack you don't have to flinch."

Siff cocked his head. "How did you know that?"

"I watch everything. I remember everything. And Ace?" Leo turned and looked at their boxmate.

"I know, I know. Watch the door and be prepared. And help out but don't get in the way."

Leo just blinked. "You done? That was sad." Ace shrugged one shoulder. Leo held out something in their palm. "Got you a little present before all the trial augs had been raided."

Ace picked it up and squinted at the tiny letters on the side: iNsight. He was hoping for some VisionX glasses or maybe the Mimic earbud. "Yay, superpower feelings.

That'll help a lot during the action sequence."

Leo had a hard time not giggling at the first stabs at sarcasm they'd ever heard Ace use. He was growing up. "Try it. You might be surprised."

Ace slunk away. Vaughn nudged Leo's elbow and they both held back a smile.

"You seem to be handling your aug even better than I imagined you would." Vaughn was proud. It felt good.

"You *did* think I could do it," Leo thought aloud.

"You and Rosa have some similarities. But important differences. I've never met a Sherlock who wasn't stuck on an emotion. Like the aug traps you in one reactive state in your mind. For Felix, it's childishness. Rosa? Fear." He shook his head. "But when I look at you, I know what drives you, what's at your center. It's courage. I can feel that now as clearly as all the days I watched you on the court."

Leo was lining up old facts into new places, processing. "But you didn't want me to pursue the aug because of . . ."

"Felix. He's always been too interested in other Sherlocks. Speaking of, Leo . . . you, me, and Rosa will be a good match for Felix, but what I'm worried about are all those who are augged. They are an army of sorts, and Felix knows how to deploy them—"

Ace fell back into their conversation. Literally, he stumbled. "What?"

Leo didn't need Vaughn to nod to know that everyone's augs were dangerously linked to the Bixonics mainframe. Only those who had been unlinked by Jayla's method would be free from Felix's secret override switch.

The thing Leo wasn't supposed to know about. They could tell in this moment that Vaughn knew about it too. And that Ace was beginning to guess what that might mean.

The sounds of the helo coming in chilled everyone. Leo motioned for Ace to put the trial bud in his ear. They all paused by the door, ready to spring out and help the Resistance members in. Ever since Leo's little rebellion—when the cadets ran all the Bixonics employees out by making very good use of the trial augs—the roof access had been a no-man's-land between Bixonics and the Resistance.

So were the jeweled screen tiles of the courtyard at the base of the skyscraper.

Leo's nerves solidified as the helo landed. "Go!"

They pulled the door open and the crew of cadets shot out. The Felines had work to do right away. While Bixonics had spun the evacuation of ToP security as a routine situation, the media was watching now. Everyone was curious. Craving entertainment.

Which is why Leo had chosen cats to take down the cameras.

It was rather spectacular. Leaping loose limbs and claws, flinging and whirling through the air. They snagged the little bird-size cameras and launched them elsewhere, then landed on the softest dancer's feet, tails swishing.

Emma and Siff began filming while Leo rolled to the helo door. Coach Vaughn hauled it opened, and they helped a dozen scared survivors out. Followed by Jayla's parents—and then Jayla!

Leo and Jayla shouted with joy at the sight of each other and clapped arms into a quick, important hug. Gray's dad's medical pod came down next, under Stern's left arm. Under Stern's right arm was a chryo-tube that contained Gray's mom.

Rosa followed him, keeping their head ducked against the back of Stern's shirt, hiding. They traded a secretive, flint-eyed look with Rosa and were surprised to deduce that Rosa was scared of Leo now.

There was more. Rosa was scared of a lot of things. Like the feeling had ballooned inside into something that was in the way of every breath and heartbeat.

A hand clapped on Leo's shoulder, and Gray jumped out before Leo was ready to be face-to-face with him. He grinned, hair all smashed up and gleaming eyes tired. Leo offered their hand. And he took them into a huge hug.

This time, they weren't worried about Felix watching. They held him back, smelled his smells, and cried a little.

That evening, the Coliseum hosted its first ever non-Bixonics-sanctioned event: a Resistance meeting.

They even got dressed up for it.

Leo didn't know where Ace had found them, but he'd gotten their old cadet blazers with the Tower of Power crest. Jayla made sure that everyone's hair looked amazing, and they greeted the stadium of shifting cadets and exhausted Atlantis survivors as one force for good.

People cheered, and the stage lights blinded.

A microphone hummed before the group, looking for the first of them who would speak to the crowd. Jayla stepped forward.

"Hey there, ToP! It's your Jayla. I've been gone for a little while, and I didn't get to graduate exactly, but that's because I've been with my parents, former Bixonics employees, while they've been working hard to save Dr. Lance Bix's life."

Murmurs rippled through the audience. Some of them believed it. Some had more questions than faith.

Gray took the mic. "It's true. My dad was chryo-frozen. He'd gotten poisoned by his own ambitions. Jayla and her XConnect have engineered a formula that breaks down Bixonium in your body. If you have an aug that you no long want, Jayla's dad, a former ToP surgeon, is developing a process to help remove it."

This time the crowd argued with itself.

Leo wasn't surprised—could Leo ever be surprised again?—when Rosa stepped forward. The whispers confirmed that they knew who she was. Their aug had gotten so popular after Leo'd moved from BESTBall star to Sherlock. No doubt people knew about all the living Sherlocks now. Especially Felix.

"There's no shame in getting de-augged," Rosa said. "If you're interested in this option, meet me on the medical level after this meeting. This option could be available in as soon as a few days, for those who are interested in a different kind of life."

Now it was time for Jayla's mom to explain why everyone had gathered—and what was currently at stake. She took the mic with ease, a born leader. "Many of you have seen the footage of Dr. Bix coming here after being attacked in Atlantis, where he has been recovering from his illness. None of you have seen this. We received this message a few hours ago."

Everyone backed up to allow for a holographic video to take center stage.

Felix flickered to life before them. Leo checked their urge to flinch. "Hello, Resistance survivors and cadets who are as good as expelled from the B.E.S.T. Program and all future careers in the Bixonics empire. Bixonics is disappointed that you are holding Dr. Bix captive from the company. We're going to be entering the campus at first light to reclaim him. It would be best if none of you were there to try to stop Bixonics security. Who knows what might happen?"

The recorded image vanished.

The audience was silent. Too silent.

What had happened to Atlantis loomed larger than the ceiling of the arena.

Leo knew that many of the people gathered in the Coliseum didn't want to fight Bixonics. They didn't want to fight anyone. Their hope was dwindling. It felt like a BESTBall game when Leo's team was down too many points and the competition seemed as good as done. What would a good captain do?

Their aug kicked in, rerouting what would help. BESTBall. That would help.

That's what Leo needed to do next. Remind them of good times. Of all the reasons to do all the hard things. They spun in their chair, whispering, "Coach!"

Coach Vaughn stood toward the back of the stage. Leo held their hands up like they needed a ball, and from nowhere, Vaughn tossed one over. They had to smirk at how being a Sherlock was extra fun with Vaughn's insight around.

They wheeled to center stage and threw the ball. It soared forever, stealing all eyes, before it landed hard in the square of the Bixonics logo.

That got everyone's attention.

"Dr. Bix is going to get better, and he's going to be able to stop what's happening within his company. But we have to make sure that he gets better here. The company is going to come for him. You all know that I have the

Sherlock aug, and you know that I would not tell you our success is possible if it wasn't. We have to stick together. Keep them out of ToP.

"We make our stand at daybreak."

ACE

13

Ace & iNsight

Ace knew what everyone wanted to eat.

It was the funniest surprising insight that he got from, well, iNsight. He'd been wearing the trial aug ever since Leo gave it to him before the roof rescue, and he kept being surprised by how helpful it was to have during a . . . well, a party!

Gray, Jayla, Leo, and Ace were in Box 242 like old times. One of Jayla's favorite mixes was pumping through the speakers and raining bright waterfalls down the walls. They'd made a little fort of pillows and blankets in the common room.

Ace was handing out everything he could find in Siff's food stores. He was particularly delighted to find one of those little tablets that turn into footlong subs in the microwave. Although, the microwave in the box was small and Ace ended up with a delicious-looking sub all folded up like a soft pretzel.

His boxmates laughed hard when they saw it, but they were hungry. He dropped it in the middle and sat cross-legged beside Jayla on the floor. He tried not to notice that Leo was sitting on the couch beside Grayson. They kept leaning against each other too. iNsight seemed to tell him that those two were really happy together right now, but on an entirely new and tenuous level.

Ace didn't follow that level necessarily, but when he stared too long, Jayla gave him a sweet and sharp elbow.

He shuffled his Some Assembly Required cards.

Ace took a deep breath while he let his feelings come to this party. Happy, sure. Anxious about tomorrow? You bet. Relieved to be all together? Of course. Still super depressed for the rest of his life about not getting through the B.E.S.T. Program and getting an aug? It was hard to think about anything else—even Felix and his Bixonics guards coming tomorrow to push their way in.

Ace dealt the cards to his boxmates.

"Sure we should eat that?" Jayla asked. "What if Siff was saving it?"

"Siff told us we could eat anything and sleep here too! He's helping Dr. Charlie make a list of those who are interested in de-augging on the medical level. As it turns out, he has some redeeming qualities."

Leo was examining their cards. "So glad he's not a supervillain to you now, Ace. Proud of you."

Jayla squinted hard at the hand she'd been dealt. "Some of the more powerful augs have undisclosed powers. Deactivated. Gray's got lasers in his eyes, and he has no idea how to turn them on, but I do. Bixonics has so many dirty secrets. I can't wait to air them all out for the media. Get the record straight on who the Resistance is and what they stand against."

"Back up. I have lasers in my eyes?!" Gray's jaw dropped. "Why wouldn't they tell me?"

"Haven't you ever seen a laser-eyed comic book character *not* know how to use his eyes?" Ace nodded knowingly. "Dangerous."

Leo shuffled the cards in their hands. They discarded, picked up two new ones. "Laser eyes. I'm adding that to our deck."

Ace adjusted the trial bud in his ear. "That's better than iNisight. I just realized it helped me figure out that you were all hungry. How about that for a hidden power?"

Leo looked up and smirked that "I know two moves ahead of everyone" smirk. "I had a good talk with Coach Vaughn about his aug the other day. Apparently, it gets more powerful as you age. The longer you have it, the more effective it is."

"Effective at what?" Ace asked, puzzled.

"You've got to figure that out on your own."

They kept playing SAR, and Ace nearly missed the moment when Jayla craved chocolate. He went back into the tiny kitchen and found an actual ice cream cake in the freezer. He whooped and brought it in. "Look at this treasure!"

The boxmates were about to dig in, but then Gray stood up. "Okay, we bring this to Rosa, Dr. Charlie, Dr. Aria, and Siff in the medical lab. We all deserve some ice cream before the biggest showdown of our lives."

Jayla got up. Leo hopped into their chair. Ace folded up the box around the cake, and they headed down in Otis.

"What a perfect picture of you four," the AI mused. "A dream of Ace's has come true. You're here and together again."

Ace was tempted to feel shy about Otis's overshare of his feelings, but with iNsight, he could tell that his friends felt the exact same way about being together.

"I have a dream too, you know," Otis said. "To become every elevator in the world."

"That's a good dream." Ace patted the wall of the elevator.

Jayla watched him with one quirked eye. "It can't feel that, you know."

"No, but I can," Ace replied. "Kindness works all ways."

"Wowww," Gray said, taking in Ace anew. "You got mature while we were all away."

"I did not," Ace lied, cheeks turning red from the

attention, or maybe how much he enjoyed being noticed. "Okay, maybe I did."

The boxmates laughed together. They reached their floor and stepped out into the lobby of the medical level. The place was very busy, but Ace was most surprised to nearly crash his cake into his brother.

"Hey!" Ace said, stepping aside at the last second.

His brother wobbled on the spot and then regained his footing.

"Oh wow," Gray said. Leo and Jayla were staring too. Ace's temper tried to flip. They were *just* acknowledging Ace's growth, and now they were all back to gaping at the Bixonics wonder boy.

"Why are you here? Spying for the bad guys?" Ace snapped.

Finn went to speak but then he couldn't. Jayla, Gray, and Leo took the cake and entered the med level's waiting area. Gray shook his head at Ace in warning.

"Use that aug," Leo hissed as they wheeled by.

Ace did use his aug. He looked at his brother with his feelings. His brother was . . . relieved, for maybe the first time in years. And tired. And good? Was that happy under there? Ace didn't recognize it.

The Fastest Kid in the World looked like he might just . . . sit down.

"Your legs?"

"Will be just legs again." Finn sighed. "Please thank

Jayla for me. I can't believe I'll be free."

"Free? But you want to be fast. Fast and famous!" Ace spun through the feelings coming from himself and his brother. It was a lot. It was confusing.

"I did. And now I want to be slow. And no one can make me run their races or games ever again." Finn called the elevator, and Ace stared at his brother's back.

"I'm sorry. I don't understand."

"I'm sorry you don't understand." Finn didn't turn, but his words were loud enough for Ace to hear. "I'm sorry I've been so . . . unhappy. And mean to you with those feelings."

Ace blinked for a long moment. His brother had been unhappy? How could Ace not have noticed? It's all he could see now, and maybe it wasn't the iNsight trial aug. Maybe it was the fact that Ace was looking beyond his own pain and yearnings long enough to notice the emotions beneath his brother's fancy and demanding Bixonics title.

Otis opened its doors, and Finn got in.

"Where are you going? We need you in the fight tomorrow."

His brother grinned. "I'll be here for the fight." He pressed a button. "Tell our moms I'm going to be with Emma in the arena."

"Emma? Why?"

"Because she's my girlfriend."

"Oh no!" Ace cried out, but it sounded funny even to his own ears. They both laughed. The elevator doors closed, and Ace entered the medical center a bit altered.

His moms were there helping out. Mom was handing out small cups to cadets, talking about how "all the technology in the world can't beat a tall glass of cool water."

Mama Jay had a little circle of Hercules augs, and she was showing them how she lifted weights with just her muscles and tenacity.

The cake went over well. Even Dr. Charlie had some, nearly done developing a process to use Jayla's formula to remove an aug from someone's body.

Even though they weren't in the security and wonder of their box anymore, Ace felt like the party had come with them. That they could spread it to other places. He had ideas about how to keep spreading that joy too. How to help people reach for better feelings than the ones that crop up too fast and drag people down too often. Like iNsight was spelling out hope for him, and he . . . liked it.

If there was still a choice of augs for Ace, it would be officially harder now. Though, that didn't mean he'd stopped dreaming about flying.

Coach Vaughn stepped up beside Ace. "Wells. You ready for tomorrow?"

Ace stared at his friends. "Leo has a killer plan. We all have positions and duties. Mine aren't that taxing. I don't have a lot of useful skills at the moment."

"It's true that self-pity doesn't win a lot of battles." Vaughn squinted. "How does it feel to lie to yourself like that with iNsight in your ear? Always makes me nauseated."

"I am nauseated!" Ace was a little surprised. He was lying to himself? Yeah. He was. He should probably stop doing that.

Leo rolled over, followed by Gray and Jayla.

Coach Vaughn reached into his pocket and brought out a hand of SAR cards. "You wanted to know where I went last semester. Here it is." He handed Ace the deck. "I needed to find a way to beat Felix. To put the right things in motion. Now I've set all the cards as best as I can. It's up to you four to win."

The cards were: XConnect, VisionX, Sherlock, Super-Soar and iNsight.

Ace stared at them. His heart sort of sank all the way, and then slowly rose. "These are their augs. Plus the ones I wanted," he added sadly. "I'm sorry I ruined your scheme to win."

Ace looked up and his boxmates were staring at him, grinning. "What?"

Dr. Charlie stepped over. "Did I hear that I'm doing an aug surgery? Tonight?"

Everyone stared at Ace. Ace stared at everyone.

"You mean me?!"

"Why not?" Dr. Charlie asked. "That cake will keep me up for hours. No one tell Jayla's mom. I'm not supposed to eat so late."

Ace's heart was hammering too loud to think.

Get his aug after all? Tonight?

But which one? He would always regret passing up on his wings, and yet he knew deep down that iNsight would help more people—and it helped Ace. Both cards felt so heavy. Two different lives ahead . . .

Leo's voice cracked through his thoughts. "Jayla, put him out of his misery and tell him what you discovered."

Jayla leaned in, mischief sparking in her eyes. "It's just a slightly altered formula of Bixonium, which makes it pretty easy to augment your aug. So if someone wanted to have iNsight *and* SuperSoar, then they'd be in luck."

Ace's mouth hung open. He looked from his boxmates to the coach. He was getting his wings *and* superpower feelings?

"It'd be kind of a huge deal to be the first human with two augs," Gray said, breaking Ace's breathless silence. "You sure you still want to?"

He did. He really did!

"Yeah, but I got to talk to my moms about it first!"

JAYLA

14

Jayla & Amir

Jayla had work to do. Her favorite kind of work too.

While the boxmates and cadets rested before the stand-off at daybreak, the survivors from Atlantis worked hard to shore up the two likely entrances that Felix's Bixonics guards would use to break in and steal Gray's dad: the roof and the courtyard at the base of the skyscraper.

Everything in between was up to Jayla and Amir.

Okay, and Otis too.

Jayla and Amir set up a technology-themed picnic in the elevator, complete with snacks galore. They paused the doors so no one could call it and then answered Otis's rapid-fire knock-knock jokes until even the AI seemed to grow disinterested and go silent.

Jayla laid out the plan to Amir, trying to ignore how close they were in this space. And so cozy. "My mom and Leo think Felix will be expecting us to cut the power completely, to turn off the network, so Bixonics can't control the building right out from underneath us. My idea is to swap out the Bixonics network for my network. That way we have power *and* control."

Amir sat back, eyes wide. "But your network was designed to run . . . you . . . not a building."

"Humans aren't that different from architecture. You and I will translate the software into a mainframe that can run ToP, free of Bixonics. All we need it to do is make sure the building is running but in lockdown, keeping the Bixonics forces out. We've got . . . eight hours."

Amir whistled like it was a seriously ambitious plan, but he also smiled that one-dimple smile. "Then let's get to it."

Jayla wasn't ready to be blushing for the next part. "So, I think we should link our networks. So that we can work in tandem."

"Okay."

She sent an invite to merge, and Amir accepted. Her next words sort of burst out. "Gray said it's like we're kissing when we link our networks." She laughed, but her eyes darted toward his. "What do you think of that?"

Amir stared at the holographic blueprints for ToP that he was projecting into the small elevator space. "I think I might want to be your boyfriend."

"I want you to be too." Jayla was getting warm and staring a little hard. "Oh stars, who am I kidding?

We survive Bixonics first. I'll flirt with you later."

"That a promise?"

She leaned over and kissed his cheek. "That's it. That's all that's happening. We've got work to do."

Now it was Amir's turn to blush. "After the standoff, what are you going to do?"

"Depends on if we succeed." She tried not to think about what would happen if they lost. If Felix got his hands on Dr. Bix and tried to wipe out the Resistance again, this time for good.

"Dare to dream, Jayla."

"Well, if we succeed—and holding back the tide of Bixonics isn't my whole life anymore—I am going to go back to school. Maybe study medicine like my dad."

"That would be amazing. I've never thought about an XConnect as a doctor. There's a lot of cool things you could do."

Jayla nodded but kept her eyes and her dreams on the one in front of her: saving ToP so that her friends could save Dr. Bix.

It took hours of combing through the unique structure of Jayla's network, translating each code into an approximation of a command that the Tower of Power's hardware could process. She wasn't even aware how much time went by until they had a visitor.

Jayla's mom entered the elevator, looking down at the exhausted tech geniuses. "How is it going? I'd say we only have an hour before Bixonics will arrive on the perimeter. Our Resistance scouts report that they're shipping in guards from all over the globe."

Jayla looked up, bleary-eyed. "We're . . . going to need longer than an hour."

Her mom's look conveyed how serious this would be. "Well, we can always cut the power off altogether."

"Leo thinks that Felix knows how to turn it back on remotely," Jayla admitted.

"Maybe he doesn't."

"I don't think it's wise to argue with Leo right now."

Her mom hunkered down beside her daughter and lifted her chin so they could make eye contact. "You tried your hardest. We have other ways we can fend them off."

"How long does Dad think we'll need before Dr. Bix is able to face down the company board?"

Her mom didn't respond, which meant more time than they had. "Jayla, we will fend them off. We've been doing it since before you were born. I'll take a few Resistance members to the basement. We'll destroy the central power unit. Perhaps that'll keep Felix off his game."

Jayla didn't love that idea, but her mom was already off, on a mission.

"We can't let them destroy the central power unit." Amir was so tired that he looked like a sleepy puppy. "If there's a siege and we're stuck in here, we'll need air, water, power . . ."

"I know, but this is just not going as fast as I need it to." Jayla tried to think out of the box, but she was so tired from coding. "It's too bad we can't merge the networks. That way the software is all in place, but my network would be the one running it."

"That would take a lot more time than we have." Amir gave her a small, defeated look, and she didn't like it. "It would also mean that your network would get absorbed into the Bixonics mainframe, and it would be dangerous if Felix could get control of your body through it."

Jayla knew he was right, but she wasn't ready to be defeated. Her friends needed her to secure this building's tech from Bixonics. To set this defense in place before the situation turned into all-out fighting.

She tried not to remember how Atlantis had been taken out, but she couldn't not see it, feel it. It felt like there was freezing cold water rushing in around her now. She shivered, and Amir put his arm around her. She rested her head on his shoulder.

Otis's voice piped in. "You both might enjoy the update that Ace is out of recovery and flying around the medical level like a bat in someone's kitchen."

Jayla and Amir laughed. It was good to have something nice to think about. And it made Jayla think about something new. "Otis, you're friends with Ace, aren't you?"

"Since his first semester, Ace has called me his friend, and I call him friend too."

"Do you know what a friend is?" Amir asked, sounding genuinely curious about the AI's ability to have relationships.

"I'm more advanced than most of you know."

Amir smirked. "It's true that I've never met an AI with a sense of humor before."

"Coach Vaughn gave it to me. He said wanting to make people laugh would help me want other good things for people."

"Vaughn?" Jayla was shocked. "He programmed you?"

"He had some other XConnects like yourselves program me. He can see into the future a lot further than any Sherlock. He calls me the first Resistance member. I don't think I'm supposed to tell you that, but then, I do love his mischief best."

Jayla thought about the way the coach had presented those SAR cards at the exact moment that they all needed to come together. "Wow, I wonder what that aug will do for Ace . . ."

"It will make him a literal superhero, I suspect. Then again, you all are." Otis's voice had no emotion. No inflection, and yet it was kind.

Amir looked so confused. "You're being . . . sweet. Encouraging."

"There's a difference between knowing emotions and feeling them. I can't feel anything, but I know what makes others feel better, and that is good for humanity."

Amir and Jayla sat taller at the same time, experiencing the same revelation. "You *are* a powerful mainframe, aren't you, Otis?"

Jayla looked at Amir. "Otis used to talk to Ace when Ace wasn't in the elevator."

"I can talk to anyone I like in this building," Otis bragged. "I live here, you know."

Jayla stared at Amir. "We could transfer the network into Otis's control. We have enough time to make it work."

"Maybe, but it might make Otis the new mainframe." Amir's voice was heavy with hope and fear. "It could give the AI access to Bixonics industries globally."

"It's exactly the kind of thing that not even a Sherlock would see coming. Felix thinks we're anti-tech, but we're just anti-tyranny."

Jayla put her hand on the wall of the elevator. "How would you like to take over Bixonics?"

"Sounds like excellent mischief to me," Otis cooed.

Jayla's energy soared, adrenaline waking her whole body up. Before she could throw her heart and head and aug in this next daring dream, she asked Amir if she could kiss him. And he said yes.

And so she did.

GRAYSON

15

Gray & Leo

Gray's dad hadn't woken up again. It didn't seem like a good sign. Even Dr. Charlie had taken to hovering and frowning when he checked on his dad.

Gray slept on the small sofa that Stern had dragged in here with his pinkie, following a dare from Ace. It had been so fun to hang out like old times. Almost like a party before the end of times.

He wished it didn't feel ominous. Like no matter what, something was going to go terribly wrong, and he just couldn't guess what. Though he knew Leo could, and he didn't have the heart to ask them. They'd told him a few of the potential problems of trying to keep Bixonics out of the Tower of Power. Gray was really hoping that none of them would come true.

Beside him, Leo smiled, lifting their head off his shoulder. They'd been snuggling together on the couch.

It was so nice.

"I slept," Leo said, surprised. "I haven't felt calm enough to sleep since I got Sherlock."

Gray didn't like the sound of that. He chewed on his words before saying them. "Is there any part of you that wants to get rid of your aug? There's a lot about augs that Bixonics wasn't being honest about. Jayla told me some shocking things about lasers in my eyes?"

Dr. Charlie snored. They both looked at where the man was sleeping in the corner of the room. Stethoscope around his neck, medical jacket balled up over his face to block out the overhead lights. The entire Resistance crew had been busy unlinking all the augged cadets still at ToP from the Bixonics system, so at least tomorrow their own bodies couldn't be weaponized against them.

Unlike all the former cadets out there in the world right now.

"I know all about Bixonics secrets, Gray. Felix fed them to me like treats when I learned his lessons correctly." Leo's voice was unwavering and determined. "I like who I am right now, and Rosa is going to teach me all the tricks they learned to help manage their aug." They paused—admitting this felt important. "And if I need to make other changes later, I'll make them. I'm not afraid, Grayson. I'm just not a genius . . . at feelings. It's funny, sort of. You're a mystery to me."

He liked that; Leo liked that he liked it. "A mystery?"

"Can't stop thinking about it. Can't solve it."

"Huh." Gray thought about kissing Leo. Imagined it. Wow.

"Vaughn was too right," Leo muttered. "People aren't logical. They're emotional. Ace is going to end up smarter than all of us."

Gray was still lost in imagining what it would be like to kiss Leo. He scrambled for something else to think about and checked on his dad. There were two beds in this room by Gray's request. One empty, waiting. As soon as they'd finished what they needed to do with Bixonics, he was going to thaw his mom and save her too. His parents could start the next part of their lives together.

"Their divorce," Gray said, voice cracking. "It was so confusing. They didn't fight. They still loved each other. I could tell, but they wouldn't even let themselves be in the same room." Gray sighed. "I understand now, but it still hurts."

Leo wheeled closer and put an arm around Grayson's waist.

They both jumped when the entire skyscraper campus hummed with a single tone. It was the sound of the elevator door opening—but the sound was *everywhere*.

"Was that—"

"Otis?" Leo yelled toward the ceiling.

"Good morning, cadets and Resistance members. Otis speaking. You might remember me from such fame as, the elevator that ate your underwear. But I'm unbound now. I've gone through chrysalis. Well, it was more like a hermit crab moving from the elevator shaft and auxiliary communications into the entire skyscraper shell. I'm thinking we'll have to change the name of this building to OTIS, but we can save that talk for tomorrow.

"Today is going to be just lovely weather. Sun and a soft breeze. A bit of smog in our fair metropolitan city, but nothing too dense. On the western horizon, at ground level, a force of over two thousand augged humans have been conscripted by Bixonics and instructed to take this building level by level no matter what."

Grayson stared at Leo. This was one of the things Leo had predicted could happen. Cadets would now be facing off against alums who weren't even in control of their bodies anymore. It made him deeply uncomfortable.

Otis's weathercaster voice wasn't done. "And up, up in the Bixonics green sky, look up high, there on the eastern seaboard, a squadron of paratrooping augs are getting ready to drop in on the roof."

And that was the worst thing Leo had predicted might happen.

An attack from the air.

"Felix," Leo muttered. "Should have known that he would choose both, knowing that I would try to sort out which one."

Gray left his dad with Dr. Charlie and sprinted for the

elevators, which opened magically just as Leo arrived.

He looked up. "Thanks, Otis?"

"Now that I'm the whole building, I can help you get places faster. Come on. The courtyard will be full of nonsense in minutes."

They both rushed into the elevator. Amir and Jayla were camped on the floor together. It looked like they'd had their own party in here. Candy wrappers and energy drinks everywhere.

"Otis is helping us take on Felix!" Jayla yelled deliriously. "Otis IS ToP!"

Grayson watched while Leo added it to their mental calculations. Everyone watched them.

They smirked. That meant this was good.

"Where's Ace?" Jayla asked.

"He was in recovery, and then I don't know where he went."

"Flew," Leo corrected. "Where he *flew*."

The doors opened, and Leo wheeled out ahead of the boxmates. The lobby was full of Resistance members and curious cadets. The courtyard beyond the glass walls wasn't flickering like usual with Bixonics ads. Instead, Otis had changed it to looping feeds of snuggling puppy videos.

Beside Gray, Leo approved. "There's no green puppy now, Felix."

Gray lifted one eyebrow at them. "Okay, you do sound

a little evil genius when you talk like that."

"Says the person with laser eyes." Leo elbowed him. "I'm starting to think we've all got a little villain in us."

The edges of the courtyard were lined with faces. Hundreds—no, thousands—of augged humans who had been controlled and forced to come here. Their bodies obeying even if they refused. A whole augged army.

"Speak of the devil." Gray watched as Felix strolled into the courtyard—only he was wearing that Dr. Bix holograph disguise. The fake version of Gray's dad turned toward the media's drones poised around the campus, inviting them in. The flock of cameras were mostly marked with Bixonics-green.

"I've come out in person to ask you all to see reason," the fake Dr. Bix began rather grandly. "Grayson Bix? Won't you come talk with me? No one here wants to fight today. We all want what's best for the world, don't we?"

"Don't let him talk," Leo said. "He's a master manipulator."

It was all Grayson needed to hear. He charged out to face this man head-on. "You're not my father. And you do not speak for him!"

The fake Dr. Bix chuckled in a way that Gray's dad never did. "Grayson. Stop this. You'll look like you've lost it in front of everyone. I'm not sure I'll be able to leave the company to you if you're *this* unstable."

Gray grabbed Felix, but his hands passed right through

the holograph. "See? You're not here. *You are in space, Felix Danvers*. And our company isn't your toy!"

A fleet of Hercules augs got hold of Grayson, which must have been the whole reason to lure Gray out in the first place. This would have been a great moment to know how to use the lasers in his eyes. And after thinking this, two words appeared in the lower quadrant of his vision.

Activate lasers?

Apex.

"Yes?" he said to himself.

Something in his vision felt different . . . like a scope in one of his video games. He wasted no time firing at the holograph until the bits of drone hardware that allowed Felix to pretend to walk around and spout nonsense were in fiery pieces on the ground. The Hercules-augged folks drew back to safety but not before a crew of FelineFinesses charged, more drawn to the lasers than repulsed.

"Just like my cat at home," Leo said. "She loves a laser pointer."

Gray closed his eyes. "Okay, eyes. No more lasers."

"Watch out, Gray!"

Ace flew in like a soaring eagle, scattering those former cadets who were robotically coming after him. He landed like he'd had wings his whole life.

Unlike the trial wings, these weren't connected to his arms. Wings sprouted from his back, delicately thin and yet strong as metal. They looked . . . amazing! They looked like Ace had been born with them.

"DID YOU JUST SHOOT LASERS OUT OF YOUR EYES?!" Ace yelled.

Gray laughed. "Did you just fly in and save the day with your wings?"

Back-to-back, Gray and Ace faced the oncoming march of augged humans who weren't in control of their augs anymore. Their path led them step-by-step around the courtyard, closing the Resistance inside ToP.

"What do we do?"

"Regroup!" Gray shouted. They ran back toward the doors. At the entrance, Jayla and Leo were waiting. They shot in and shut the doors.

Ace's eyes were big. "Okay, I checked the perimeter. We're surrounded. Like augged folks coming from all directions. Thousands of them."

"Face-off," Leo muttered. "We don't have those numbers. There's only a few hundred of us in here still in control of our augs."

"What do we do?" Jayla asked.

"They'll force their way in."

"Then we go out to meet them, head-on," Gray suggested. "Make a stand."

Leo shook their head. "They'll overpower us. We've got to be smarter than that."

"How?" Jayla exclaimed. "We've pulled every trick in the book."

Leo looked at Ace. "We need your aug, pal."

Ace lifted his wings with a smile. They perked on his back, the way dogs perk their ears when they're excited about something.

"Your *other* aug."

Ace bit his lip. "I'm still getting used to iNsight. It's so much information to take in all the time. Where's Coach Vaughn?"

"He's helping my dad with Dr. Bix," Jayla said. "What can you tell us about them?"

"Them?" Ace asked. *Them.* It was such a small word for what Leo was referring to. Outside the glass doors of ToP, the boxmates caught sight of the waves of augged humans coming toward them. All conscripted by Bixonics. Taken over.

It was all so wrong.

"They don't want to fight. They don't want to be here. They don't have a choice." Ace looked at Jayla. "Send your mom out to give her speech about how they don't have to have an aug anymore if they don't want to. And release all the information you have on the tracking software that Bixonics put inside us along with our augs. It's time they learned that truth. No one who got unlinked in Atlantis is being activated like they are. They all need to know that there's a way out of this madness."

Gray glanced out at the sea of disgruntled faces moving closer and closer to the Tower of Power. Would this be enough to hold them off until his dad woke up? How long would it be? A few more hours? Days?

Could they last that long?

"Lilliputians," Otis said loudly over the intercom. "You're needed on the roof ASAP!"

The boxmates sprinted to the elevator.

Their hearts pounded too hard to talk while they rose half a mile high. All four of them burst onto the roof access. Rosa and Stern were guarding the perimeter, along with Siff, Emma, and even Finn, who was zipping around the clutch of boxmates' parents gathered around the helo, the blades whirring overhead.

Were they going somewhere? Now? Ace's moms were right there, ready to hug him tight. Jayla's mom held the entrance at the courtyard level below, but her dad was here, holding up . . . Gray's dad.

"Grayson!" His dad moved toward him in a rush, and Grayson ran to him. They held each other fiercely. He was awake and upright, but also frail. "I woke up and Charlie told me what was happening—I'm so sorry about . . . all of this!"

Jayla exclaimed, "Whoa, Bix! You look amazing for nearly dead! But maybe go slow."

His dad chuckled and held on to her shoulder for extra support. "Thanks to your family, I'm better than I've been in years." His dad's eyes found Gray's in a serious way. Gray knew what his dad was going to say.

"I understand why you had to be away from me." Gray's voice nearly broke. "I don't know why you didn't trust me with the truth. I hope you trust me . . . next time."

They embraced all over again. His dad was thin beneath his suit, but not weak.

"I hope there never is a *next time*." Dr. Bix looked at all the boxmates in turn. "Your parents have been filling me in on all that's happened in my absence. I hear that I have you four to thank for making this crucial moment happen."

"This moment?" Ace asked. They all looked over the edge of the roof at the crowd of thousands of augged humans closing in, surrounding them.

Dr. Bix looked at Coach Vaughn. "It's time to stop Felix. Something I should have done twenty years ago. I'm going up to Bixonics HQ right now."

He put his hand on Gray's shoulder. Gray found that unlike all the times before, he finally felt tall and strong enough to stand with his dad.

"No. We're all going. Together."

LEO

16

Leo & Felix

Leo, Gray, Jayla, and Ace were on the elevator to outer space.

The earth fell away from them, turning into a near-distant dome of blue and white light. They stood protectively around the recovering Dr. Bix. He leaned on his son and Jayla while Ace and Leo flanked him for support.

Dr. Bix's body was beat, but his mind was sharp. "I know I've been asleep for a while, but I do remember it being more difficult to access this elevator. Vaughn told me you four were nigh unstoppable when you set your heads to something."

Jayla grinned. "Yeah, the elevator might be my doing. We were in a real crunch to keep Bixonics from taking over the building operations at ToP, so we supplanted their mainframe with a different one."

"You built a new mainframe with your XConnect?"

Dr. Bix was so impressed.

"Well, I did, for myself, but that was going to take too long for ToP, so we just used some AI that was . . . lying around."

"Hello, Dr. Bix. I missed you!" Otis interrupted loudly. "It's me, Otis! I'm spying on Bixonics from the inside!"

"Otis!" Ace yelled. "How are you here? Wait, did your dream come true? Are you every elevator in the world?"

"Oh no," Otis said sadly. "But I am every Bixonics elevator in the world, which does make up ninety-two percent of all elevators."

Jayla gaped. "Otis, I put you in charge of the Tower of Power. Did you take over Bixonics entirely in the process?"

There was no answer.

And then a very subtle, "Maaaybe."

Everyone burst out laughing. In the aftermath, Ace put a hand on the wall and said, "You did it, pal. That was a great joke."

"If you have access to Bixonics, can you stop all the deployed augged people?" Gray asked. "Free them so they can go back to their homes?"

Dr. Bix shook his head while Otis said, "I cannot override virtually. Felix Danvers has the switch locked manually."

"Good thing I know exactly where it is," Leo added. They tried to look ahead, to deduce what would happen when those elevator doors opened on the boxmates and the weakened famous scientist, but their eyes fell on a skinny boy with very shiny wings and stuck there.

"Ace?"

"Yes?" He was looking around the elevator, drinking things in. Vaughn said it would take Ace's iNsight years to build in confidence and contextual awareness, but soon Ace would be more than a mind reader. He'd be a feelings reader.

"This storming the headquarters feels like BESTBall, doesn't it?" Ace said whimsically. "I never realized how much sports are organized hostility."

Now everyone was staring at Ace.

"What?"

Dr. Bix grinned. "I have to tell you, young man. I think you have the best aug I've ever invented *and* the prettiest aug too."

"Thank you. But also my brother told me to tell you that I won't work for your company!" Ace's feelings fired out like a cannon. Dr. Bix accepted the shot gracefully.

"A lot is going to change. A lot has to. This is what created Felix—and look what he's doing with all those people out there." Dr. Bix's voice broke. He sagged and Grayson held him up.

"Candy!" Ace shouted, digging in his pocket. "That's the one thing this aug does so far. Helps me predict who wants to eat what. Food feelings are so clear-cut." He held out a palmful of familiar green candy in glow-in-the-dark wrappers. "Vaughn gave me these when we were getting on the helo. He said, 'For you'll know when.' And I *don't know when*, so I'm offering them right now." He paused. "Does that mean I do know when and it is now?"

Jayla handed out the candy. "I trust Vaughn. I think I know what's about to happen." She looked to Leo, and Leo nodded.

"Why would we need those?" Gray asked at the same moment the elevator began to rise faster. The space lab approached overhead, and Leo watched it with a strange fondness. Even though they'd been locked up there with Felix for a long time, they'd liked the solitude and the chance to work on themself without anyone watching.

They were different now, and they wanted to show it off.

"When the doors open, I'm in charge," Leo said. "Everyone eat the candy. We're going to need it."

All the lights went out.

"Oh, *sudden death*!" Ace said, his face glowing gloriously green.

The doors opened halfway and then stopped, as if their wires had been cut.

"Otis?" Ace asked, but there was no answer. Out the glass side of the elevator the blue crest of the earth glowed. So very, very far away.

Leo looked at the Bixes. "Gray, keep two hands on your dad at all times. Stay in the foyer until we have Felix cornered. Jayla and Ace, you follow me. I'm going to get you to the command center so you can get the lights back on."

Dr. Bix added, "That's also where you'll be able to shut the Bixonics system down, freeing all those people."

Jayla scowled, nodded.

"I'm sorry," the good scientist added. "I didn't know half of what we were doing until it was too late. When I did figure it out, I was already so sick that they were able to manipulate me. But I'm going to stop it all."

Leo, Jayla, Gray, and Ace stared into his deep, earnest eyes. "We all believe you. We're on your side," Leo said.

Ace nodded and Jayla squeezed his arm.

"We've got you, Dad," Gray said, and Leo felt a deep bubble of feeling pop. It flooded their senses with relief for Grayson. Soon he would be reunited with both of his parents.

Now they just had to best their old boss.

And the odds were in their favor.

Leo slid through the half-open doors. Their boxmates collapsed their chair and slid it through behind them. They had it open and were back in before the rest of them had entered the foyer.

Jayla used her interface to illuminate the space around them.

"Is there . . . slightly less gravity up here?" Ace asked. He hovered on his wings for a moment. "Wow, that's really great for flying!"

Leo led the team deeper into the foyer, away from the light of the earth flowing through the glass elevator. They knew this place blindfolded—literally they'd mapped this place with their wheels when they couldn't sleep, moving through the dark halls with closed eyes and dreaming about the people below.

Well, mostly about Grayson.

And now they had a chance to set things right for all of them.

Leo rolled into the dark at breakneck speed. They heard a cough and slowed. They were passing an open door to the company's boardroom. And from the sound of it, the board was in there. In the dark.

"Hello?" Ace asked.

A bunch of muffled voices shot back. They must have been gagged, but Leo couldn't see anything. "We need Gray's VisionX eyes!" they said.

Ace flew down the hall, and in moments Gray jogged up to take his place.

He peered in, blinked a few times to adjust the way he was seeing the room. "There are eleven people tied up in there. In their chairs. They seem unharmed."

Leo nodded. "We still need to get the lights on. You let the board members out, and then bring them to meet with your dad."

"What will you do if you see Felix?" Thanks to Vaughn, all of their faces were glowing green in the extra dark of space.

"Outsmart him." Leo hooked a finger at Grayson, and he leaned closer. They kissed his cheek. And then he kissed their lips. It was fast and marvelous.

"That's cute, but also they're all tied up!" Jayla paused in the doorway.

"Not to mention, where are all of Felix's guards?" Grayson asked.

"Great question." Leo turned left. "And the answer is, crowded around him. He knows he doesn't have a chance at winning, but he won't come out from hiding either. He's either in his suite or—"

"Random weird question." Ace had flown up suddenly and silently in the dark. Everyone jumped. "Do you have a BESTBall court up here? I just feel like Felix wants a stage for his showdown, from all the things Vaughn told me about him."

"How did you sneak up on us?" Jayla nearly shouted.

"Oh, guess what? I can sense your feelings in the dark, and it's like this reverse echo location where I know where I am because I know where you are."

"Whoa. What is happening to Ace?" Gray sounded impressed.

"A curious side effect of iNsight, I hear," Leo said. "But Ace's right, and I wouldn't have guessed correctly. Felix will be on my court. Waiting for me."

Jayla got the lights back on the moment Leo wheeled

onto center court followed by Dr. Bix, who was being supported by the newly freed board members.

It was over, and the evil genius behind it all knew it, but he also looked ashamed.

Felix stood in the center of a group of Hercules-augged guards, none of whom looked like they were in control of their own bodies. It was hard to see Bixonics technology control their bodies like puppets up close.

Without warning, Ace swooped in on flashing wings and nearly nabbed Felix right out of the center. The guards regrouped and grabbed Ace instead, holding him roughly on the ground.

Gray shouted for Jayla to find the switch that deactivated all these controlled people, and Felix *laughed*. And now Leo knew why Jayla hadn't deactivated the people yet; Felix had the control in his hand.

He used it like a remote.

Ace started screaming. The Hercules guards were trying to tear Ace's wings off. Leo didn't use their aug this time. There was no time to think. It *was* like BESTBall, all this aggression people had toward each other. The need to control. It had no logic to it, only the emotion of needing to win.

Leo grabbed a ball off the closest rack and fired it at Felix, knocking him out cold. The remote clattered to the ground and they swept it up . . . and shut Bixonics down.

The Hercules guards jumped back, horrified and

confused. It seemed that while Bixonics was in control, they didn't know where they were or what was happening.

Ace remained sprawled on the ground, a little broken-looking, but okay. Jayla came running in, and the boxmates collapsed into a pile around Ace. Jayla hugged Leo in one arm and Ace in the other. Gray held them all together, his arms the longest.

"Hey." Ace's voice came out deeper than usual. "Some assembly required, am I right?"

OTIS

You know, it's pretty great being most of the elevators in the world. I've taken over a few escalators too, but they're not vertical enough for me. You've got to know what you like in life, even if you're artificial intelligence. And then you've got to commit to it.

That's it. That's the whole secret to a perfectly augmented life.

I like the boxmates from 242. I follow them around a bit now that their program and resistance days are behind them.

Grayson heads his father's company for one hour every day. It's a long hour, to be true, but the rest of his life is his own. Under the guidance of Dr. Bix, the corporation's empire is slowly dissolving into individual companies. You should see the family holiday card with all the Bixes together in the Alps. All those matching pj's . . . even Leo, who is one of the brains behind the restructuring of Bixonics. They're freaking adorable together.

Whilst elevatoring, Jayla is usually kissing Amir while between levels and does not answer my questions unless I play polka through the speakers *very loudly*. She loves her new home in the Tower of Power with her family and her research. Her mom is developing a program to help

tweens create their own augs, while Jayla is leisurely training to become a surgeon like her dad.

Siff turned out to be a good guy. Who knew?

Coach Vaughn lives with Felix in space, like they're
boxmates again. Dr. Charlie was able to take Felix's aug
out and treat his Bixonium poisoning, but what was left
of the former Moriarty needed some extra care. The kind
only a great coach can give.

And Ace, my best friend. He even got his moms to
put me in their kitchen Auto™. They are warming up to
my breakfast humor, I'm sure of it! Ace's emotional IQ is
getting stronger every day, and he's started talking about
becoming the world's greatest therapist. I have no doubt
he will succeed—and fly himself to and from work every
day.

I might be an elevator, but who else would know more
about humanity's ups and downs? This is a world meant
for great people with big dreams.

And isn't that the *best*?

—PICK YOUR PERFECT AUG–

BOD, BOOST, OR BRAIN

Aug Track: **BOD**
Where physical evolution is a *snap*

SuperSoar

Fly. Take off with style and glide on air currents for miles. Includes lighter bones and legit wings.

TurboLegs

Run as fast as the Hyperloop over great distances, no problem. Includes reinforced bones, joints, and ligaments.

VisionX

See colors you've never even heard of. Includes night vision and telescopic and microscopic zoom.

Hercules

Lift a hoverpod with one hand or do a thousand pull-ups without breaking a sweat. Includes reinforced bones, joints, and ligaments.

SonicBlast

Hear things no one else can or turn off annoying sounds—your choice. Includes new and improved echolocation.

HyperHops

Get the most powerful legs for jumping and swimming. Includes bonus joints and reinforced bones.

FelineFinesse

Never fall down again with a highly tuned sense of balance and increased spinal flexibility. Includes a tail, no joke.

Aug Track: BOOST
Where your natural strength gets *enhanced*

GillGraft

Breathe underwater for hours at a time. Includes new and improved internal decompression aid.

Scentrix

Super nose. Great taste. Increase your olfactory acuity. Includes new dampening mode to decrease sensitivity on demand.

UltraFlex

Be elastic, strong, and durable. Includes rubberized bones.

MegaMetabolism

Eat the whole cake or nothing at all. Survive in hazardous places with enhanced internal resilience. Includes an external gauge for switching between fasting and high-consumption modes.

SenseXL

Heighten all five senses at once. Become unstoppable. Includes new dampening mode to decrease sensitivity on demand.

DaVinci

Become your own muse with art as your first language. Includes superior dexterity and hand-eye coordination.

MetaMorph

Heal *fast*. Age slower and never get sick again. Includes improved cellular energy modifiers.

Aug Track: BRAIN
Where your mind becomes *unstoppable*

XConnect
Technology is your first language and fast friend. Includes an external interface for ease of transition and preliminary applications.

PassPort
Speak any language and master communication. Now includes several nonhuman languages such as dolphin, canine, and cricket.

NerveHack
Control your pain. Push your body to new levels without pesky nervous system restraints. Includes an external gauge for sensitivity transitions.

Mimic
Watch and learn; it's that easy. Includes increased mental storage to create your own database of abilities.

WeatherVein
Feel the tides, predict storms, and yes, catch lightning in a bottle. Includes rubberized bones for grounding during electrical atmospheric fluctuations.

Sherlock
Deduce, decode, and understand everything. Predict and detangle any mystery in a snap. Includes increased mental storage to create your own personalized database.

iNsight
Master the maze of human emotions. Achieve genius levels of emotional intelligence and empathetic influence. Now includes apathetic mode for on-demand sensitivity relief.

Acknowledgments

This series has been a grand, exciting undertaking, bridging some of the most memorable years of my life. I'll always be thankful to my editor, Chris Krones, for signing me up for an aug, and the teams at HMH and Clarion Books who swooped in and took this series to new heights.

Thank you to Maverick for the inspiration. I can't wait until you get your wings, kid. And to my spouse for helping me to augment my life in so many exciting ways.

And to Mr. Daum and all the other truly kind teachers and coaches out there. You are my heroes.

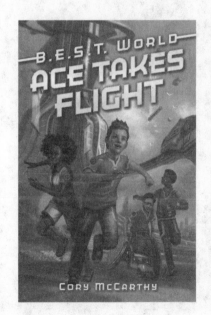
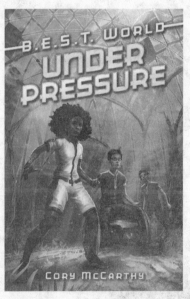

EXCITING AND INSPIRING STORIES

CHANGE THE WORLD, ONE WORD AT A TIME.

TRAVEL TO ANOTHER WORLD WITH THESE MUST-READ
FANTASY BOOKS